THE HIDDEN WORLD OF
Changers

No. 7: The Spider's Curse

by H. K. Varian

Simon Spotlight

New York London Toronto Sydney New Delhi

This book is a work of fiction. Any references to historical events, real people, or real places are used fictitiously. Other names, characters, places, and events are products of the author's imagination, and any resemblance to actual events or places or persons, living or dead, is entirely coincidental.

SIMON SPOTLIGHT
An imprint of Simon & Schuster Children's Publishing Division
1230 Avenue of the Americas, New York, New York 10020
This Simon Spotlight edition July 2017
Copyright © 2017 by Simon & Schuster, Inc.
Text by Laurie Calkhoven
Illustrations by Tony Foti
All rights reserved, including the right of reproduction in whole or in part in any form.
SIMON SPOTLIGHT and colophon are registered trademarks of Simon & Schuster, Inc.
For information about special discounts for bulk purchases, please contact Simon & Schuster
Special Sales at 1-866-506-1949 or business@simonandschuster.com.
Designed by Nick Sciacca
The text of this book was set in Celestia Antiqua.
Manufactured in the United States of America 0617 FFG
10 9 8 7 6 5 4 3 2 1
ISBN 978-1-4814-9826-5 (pbk)
ISBN 978-1-4814-9827-2 (hc)
ISBN 978-1-4814-9828-9 (eBook)
Library of Congress Catalog Card Number 2016952972

Impundulu

Hailing from the southern tip of Africa, the impundula is a massive bird of prey that can control the weather at will, summoning fearsome storms.

Its immense wingspan and connection to the weather has made this Changer a master of the skies. With a flap of its wings, the impundula can cause a powerful gust of wind or an earth-shattering clap of thunder. Lightning bolts can be channeled through the body and redirected with its talons.

Though the ability is rare, powerful impundulus can generate electricity within themselves. This energy can be used in the Changer's human form to create force fields and fire off lightning bolts whenever needed. For this reason, the impundula is perhaps the most powerful fighter both on land and in the sky.

Prologue

Darren Smith scrolled through websites about South African tribal mythology on his laptop, trying not to worry about his friend Makoto "Mack" Kimura. But worried thoughts kept creeping in anyway.

Up until their first day of seventh grade at Willow Cove Middle School, Mack and Darren had barely been acquaintances. They nodded to each other in the halls, sure, but they hung out with different crowds.

Then everything changed on the first day of seventh grade when Darren learned that he and Mack, along with fellow classmates Fiona Murphy and Gabriella Rivera, were members of a small and very secret group of people with magical powers—magical *shape-shifting* powers.

The four kids were part of a line of magical beings called Changers. Changers had the power to transform into creatures the human world believed were mythological. Darren and the others had learned that those mythological creatures were, in fact, very, very real.

Darren discovered that he was an *impundulu*, a fearsome bird that could shoot lightning bolts from its razor-sharp talons and create violent storms. Gabriella was a *nahual*, a powerful jaguar with yellow eyes, sleek jet-black fur, and the ability to spirit-walk in other people's minds. Fiona was the daughter of the *selkie* queen, a seal that ruled the oceans. With her *selkie* cloak Fiona could transform into a seal herself, and the *selkie* songs she learned from her mother contained potent magic. And Mack was a *kitsune*, a powerful white fox with paws that blazed with fire, just like his grandfather.

The four young Changers trained together every day at school and formed a close bond. Darren's new friends were the people who got Darren through those confusing early days when he was coming into his powers. Learning about his abilities and finding out that his parents were getting a divorce at the same time had almost been too much to bear. He couldn't tell his family about his secret powers, but his big brother, Ray, knew all about what it was like to be different. He and Darren were among just a few African American kids in Willow Cove.

I wish I could tell Ray just how different I am, Darren thought, not for the first time. *He could help me make sense out of all this.*

He would have loved to talk to Ray about his new abilities, but Darren had been warned against it. Changers once lived openly alongside humans. In fact, Changers did their best to protect humans from dark forces. But a long time ago humans came to believe that Changers wanted to destroy them. Changer magic frightened them, and that fear made them act in desperate, dangerous ways. The Changers had been forced to create a hidden world. They were still devoted to protecting humans from evil, but now they did it in secret and from a distance.

The First Four, leaders of all Changer-kind, had begun training Darren and the other three Willow Cove

Changers. Mack's grandfather, Akira Kimura, and his friends steered them in the discovery and control of their new powers. Dorina Therian, a werewolf, was the kids' primary coach. Yara Moreno, an *encantado*, or dolphin Changer, and Sefu Badawi, a *bultungin*, or hyena Changer, stepped in to help when they were needed. And it seemed they were very much needed, because lately, dark magic had ensured that they were constantly in touch.

Things got even more confusing when Darren and his friends learned that an ancient prophecy had foretold that *they* would become the next First Four. One day they would take over leadership of the Changer world from Mr. Kimura and the others. That also meant they had targets on their backs.

Not all of the magic community was as protective of humans as the First Four. The young Changers, or younglings as the Changer-world called them, had been forced to come together to battle and defeat a powerful warlock named Auden Ironbound. They had just accomplished that when a new dark force began to target them—an evil *kitsune* named Sakura, also known as the Shadow Fox.

The Shadow Fox was a memory eater. She could consume whatever memories she wanted, and in doing so, she could also absorb that Changer's powers. A former student of Mr. Kimura's, she had left him to delve into dark magic and then turned on him when that went very, very wrong. She had long been underground, watching and waiting for the right moment to take her revenge.

Recently, she had come out of hiding. Sakura was determined to wage a war with those who supported the First Four—a war for control of magical and nonmagical beings. To do that, she needed followers—followers who came willingly as well as followers who were forced to do so.

Her first target was Mack. Sakura poisoned Mack's mind with dark magic. She lured him away from the group with promises of evil power. She turned his happiness and hope into anger and despair. Mack was helpless while under her control, and so, he had joined her dark forces.

It had been over a month since Mack disappeared with Sakura and a week since school let out for the summer. To avoid questions, the First Four had blocked memories of Mack from the minds of everyone in Willow Cove.

Darren understood why the First Four had to do that. They couldn't exactly tell the world that Mack had been kidnapped by an evil Changer. But erasing him from the memories of the nonmagical people who knew him still didn't feel right.

Mack isn't someone who can be erased, Darren thought. *Even if the rest of our classmates don't remember him, they have to feel the hole he left behind. I know I do.*

Mack's best friend, Joel Hastings, reinforced that belief. Every time Darren passed Joel in the hallways at school, the poor guy looked superlonely. Magic might have blocked Joel's memories of Mack, but part of him knew that something was missing. Darren could tell. That last day at school, during lunch period, Darren had tried to talk to him.

"Joel!" he'd called out as he sat down across from him in the caf.

"Huh?" Joel had said, his expression blank. "Oh—hey, Darren. What's up?"

"Not much—how'd the art fair go last week?"

"Fine, but it's so weird," Joel had said with a shake of his head. "A few weeks before the deadline, I realized I only had half of the project done. I thought I was right on schedule, but it's like half of the comic I was working on just—"

"Disappeared," Darren blurted out. Joel's words hit Darren like a punch in the gut. Mack had told him about the comic book he was illustrating with Joel for the fair. It was a project Mack hadn't been able to see through to the end.

But there was no time for crying about Mack. No time for Darren to pretend he was a normal kid planning a normal summer vacation of video games, hanging out at the community pool, or meeting his buddies for lunch at the Willow Cove Café. Instead, Darren devoted all of his time to helping the First Four in their war against Sakura.

When Mack first disappeared, they searched for him nonstop. They raided Changer base after Changer base. But every time they found one, Sakura and her forces had just abandoned it. The Shadow Fox seemed to be always one step ahead of them.

The First Four suspected that she was planning to try to get her claws into Darren next. Fiona had learned the magical *selkie* Queen's Song, and that would keep her safe from any attempts at mind control, including memory eating. Gabriella had an ancient Aztec artifact, the Ring of Tezcatlipoca, which did the same thing. But Darren had no such protection, and that left him vulnerable to Sakura's magic.

So, finally, Mr. Kimura assigned another team to the hunt for Mack while the First Four focused on finding protection for Darren. Protection from Sakura's memory eating.

Darren knew finding protection was important, but at the same time the search felt like a frustrating waste of time. Each day spent hunting for a talisman for Darren was another day that wasn't devoted to finding Mack.

What if we run out of time? Darren wondered.

Every time a *kitsune* mastered a rare power or accomplished a heroic deed, he or she earned a new tail. Mack had two tails before Sakura got her claws into him. After their encounter, he gained a shadowy third tail. They guessed that Sakura was putting her new apprentice through intense training to earn a fourth. If Mack earned one more tail using dark magic, it would be impossible to reverse the hold Sakura had on him. He'd be a villain forever, just like Sakura.

We're wasting time searching for protection for me, Darren thought. *Finding Mack is more important. Maybe I should offer to go into hiding so that the others can concentrate on Mack instead of worrying about me. I'm nothing more than a burden to them right now.*

Darren was so lost in thought that he didn't hear Ray, who was home from college for the summer, knock on his bedroom door. He jumped when Ray patted him on the shoulder.

"You left your phone downstairs," Ray said, handing Darren his cell. "A Professor Zwane from Wyndemere Academy called."

Darren tried to keep his face neutral as he took the phone. "Thanks, bro."

"So now that you might be going to a fancy boarding school, are you going to make me answer all your calls?" Ray teased. "Do you need a secretary?"

Darren laughed. "If I manage to get into a fancy

boarding school, I'll probably need a tutor," he said. "But unfortunately, I'm not related to anyone smart enough. Except Mom, I guess."

Ray summoned a look of mock outrage and managed to squeak out, "Doth mine ears deceive me? You'll be lucky if I don't school you on endothermic reactions just to embarrass you in front of the boarding school girls."

"Well, now after you've said that, you're definitely *not* hired," Darren said with a grin. "Embarrassment is cause for an immediate 'you're fired.' Now let me call this guy back, or they'll change their minds about me before I even go for a tour."

"Of course, grand pooh-bah." Ray laughed and bowed before leaving the room.

As soon as he did, Darren returned Professor Zwane's call. Professor Zwane was a Changer and a teacher at the only high school in America just for Changers. If he was calling, there had to be news.

Chapter 1
Return to Wyndemere

Professor Zwane picked up after the first ring. "Darren," he said, "I think I found something."

Darren was stunned. They'd been searching for weeks for a talisman and had come up with nothing.

If I have protection against Sakura, we can go back to doing what we should be doing anyway: searching for Mack and getting him away from the Shadow Fox before he earns another tail.

"Darren," Professor Zwane said, snapping him back into the present. "Are you still there?"

"Yeah—s-sorry," Darren stammered. "You found something that will protect me from the Shadow Fox?"

"I've found something that I think will work."

"What is it?" Darren asked.

"I don't want to talk about it over the phone—you're no doubt being watched. I'm sending Margaery Haruyama to bring you here. She's already on her way."

"I'll be ready," Darren said.

Darren knew Margaery. She was a *tengu*, a Japanese bird Changer. Unlike *impundulus*, who had the power to control lightning, *tengus* had power over the wind. They could use that power to transport anyone anywhere in the blink of an eye.

"One other thing," Darren began, a bit unsteady. "Is there any chance this spell could also—"

"I'm afraid it won't break the curse," the professor answered.

Darren had been so consumed with worries about Mack that he had nearly forgotten the startling news he had learned from Professor Zwane when he first visited Wyndemere Academy in the spring. He and his friends wouldn't be able to attend Wyndemere until the ninth grade, but Darren and the others had visited the campus.

Being on a campus full of people like him was the first time Darren didn't feel like a total freak since he found out he was an *impundulu*. Exploring Wyndemere along with Fiona, Gabriella, and Mack had been a bright spot in a long and confusing school year.

Then two things happened to dull that light: Sakura appeared and attacked Mack, and Darren found out his family was cursed.

Darren had sat in on a lecture by Professor Zwane on West and South African mythology. He hoped to learn something about his own history and get a taste of high school classes at the same time. He was totally unprepared for what the professor told him after class.

"From the minute you walked into my classroom, I could sense that your power too is bound by the Spider's Curse," Professor Zwane had told him.

Darren was so shocked by the news that he could hardly form questions, but the professor, an *impundulu* himself, shared what he knew.

In ancient times, before the Changer nation was established to prevent such things, there were sometimes wars between different magical factions. Usually, they had to do with establishing power over a particular area that was valuable for its resources or strategic for defense. A bitter conflict broke out between the spider Changers—sometimes called *anansis* after the West African trickster god—and the *impundulus*.

The professor explained that during the conflict, the *anansis* cursed many *impundulus* with a powerful poison contained in their bite. The *anansis'* poison can curse more than the individual *impundulu* they've bitten. The curse courses through the whole bloodline, passing down from generation to generation.

There had been no clear winner before a truce was finally reached between the two factions, but many of the strongest *impundulu* bloodlines were cursed. The curse suppressed the Changer gift in younglings so that generations passed without anyone in that family ever presenting Changer powers . . . without ever knowing that they themselves might be Changers if the curse weren't in place.

Feelings were high on both sides after the truce. Most *anansis* had refused to lift the curse, so it continued to modern times, and the only way a person could get the curse lifted now was to find the descendant of the original *anansi* who'd cursed him or her and have the curse broken.

Professor Zwane told him that Darren had descended from a once-cursed bloodline. For some reason, Darren's magic was powerful enough to develop, despite the *anansi* curse.

Things with Mack got out of control so fast, Darren thought. *I never even told Gabriella and Fiona about the Spider's Curse.*

Even so, the knowledge of the curse was always hovering in the back of Darren's mind, like homework he'd put off until the last minute or a test he'd forgotten to study for. At first he hoped that if he found a way to break the curse, he might discover that someone else in his family was an *impundulu*. After all, Mack had his grandfather, Fiona had her mother, and even Gabriella's aunt and grandmother were Changers. Darren longed for a family member to share his experience with.

But today his first thought wasn't about the possibility of Ray or his mother becoming an *impundulu*. His first thought was about Mack.

Darren had just ended the call when he saw a movement, like a flicker, in the air. With a *whoosh* that ruffled the papers on his desk, Margaery landed in Darren's room along with Gabriella and Fiona.

"Darren!" Fiona cried. "Can you believe it? Margaery said one of the professors at Wyndemere found a protection spell for you!"

"I know," Darren said with a smile. "We can finally get back on Mack's trail."

Behind Fiona, Darren saw Gabriella flinch slightly.

"Ready to go?" Margaery asked him, breaking the silence.

"Can you wait for me outside?" Darren answered. "I have to tell my mom I'm going out."

The group disappeared as quickly as they had arrived, and Darren bounded down the stairs. He found his mother in the kitchen.

"Hey, Mom," he called. His mom turned around from the pizza slice she was microwaving. "I just got a text from Gabriella—mind if I head over to her house? We're going to work on summer book reports."

His mother smiled at him. "You usually put that

kind of thing off until the end of the summer," she said.

Darren chuckled nervously. "What can I say? Fiona and Gabriella have been a good influence on me."

"Hey," she said, throwing up her hands in defense. "Don't let my surprise stop you from doing your home-work early."

"Don't worry, I won't," Darren said. He felt a bit guilty about the lie, but he couldn't exactly tell his mother the truth.

Bye, Mom. I'm going to travel by wind to a magical school for shape-shifters and learn how to protect myself from a crazed villain who wants to control my mind. Oh, and maybe I'll even find out how to lift the curse our family has been living under for a thousand years.

He made a mental note to get started for real on his summer book report as soon as he had the time.

"I'll pick you up around dinnertime?" his mother added.

"Sounds good," Darren answered with a nod. He headed outside and found the group in the backyard, under the tree that held his old tree house.

"Ready?" Margaery asked.

Darren nodded. He put a hand on Margaery's arm. Fiona and Gabriella did the same.

There was another *whoosh*, and for a moment all Darren felt was stillness. Then the world flew by for two or three head-spinning seconds. They landed gently in the middle of the Wyndemere Academy campus.

Darren blinked in the sunlight, then turned to the Gothic castle that served as the school's academic building. Unlike the last time they were here, the grounds were empty and quiet—almost eerie, even in the brightness of the summer sun.

Professor Zwane waited for them at the door of his office. Darren was surprised to see Sefu standing behind him. He was even more surprised to see the rest of the First Four inside. Each one of them was holding something.

"What's going on?" Darren asked.

"I met with a very old *impundulu* from Pretoria last week," Professor Zwane said. "He told me about an ancient warrior protection spell that predates the written language. No wonder I didn't find it in any of my books. It may be just what you need."

Fiona walked over to the papers on the professor's desk. "What language is this?" she asked.

"A tribal language," the professor told her. "It hasn't been spoken since ancient times, and there was never a written alphabet. But parts of it did evolve into many modern languages. The *impundulu* I met with is one of the few beings who still knows how to speak it."

Seeing Fiona's confusion, Professor Zwane added one last detail. "I recorded the *impundulu*'s words using the Latin alphabet."

Darren stifled a groan. He could tell that Fiona was about to ask another question about the ancient language, and Fiona's intellectual curiosity would appeal to the professor. That could easily turn into a long discussion about the evolution of language, and Darren didn't want to take the time for a lecture right now. He wanted to hear about the spell.

Gabriella must have had the same thought. She jumped in before Fiona had the chance to ask another question.

"This spell will protect Darren from Sakura?" Gabriella asked. She bounced on the balls of her feet the same way she did when she was on the soccer field, impatiently waiting for the ball.

"This spell draws on the power of all of Darren's ancestors to guard and protect him," the professor said.

"We think it will protect him from Sakura's mind control," Mr. Kimura added.

Darren couldn't help but see the sadness and worry in the man's eyes. "So we can start looking for Mack again," he said.

Mr. Kimura nodded. "Yes, so we can resume our search for Makoto."

Yara handed a jar of something terrible-smelling to Professor Zwane. "I have the blue whale's milk you asked for," she said.

I hope she didn't have to milk a whale, Darren thought.

Sefu gave the professor what looked like a dried spice. "Red sand from the deserts of Babylon," he said.

Ms. Therian produced a rare savanna herb.

Finally, Mr. Kimura handed the professor an ivory bowl covered in ancient runes.

Darren had thought they were just going to learn about the spell. The idea of actually doing it was suddenly overwhelming. Like everything else in the Changer world, things were moving just a bit too fast for him.

"We're doing it now?" he asked. "Right now?"

Are all of my ancestors going to appear? he wondered. *Am I going to be surrounded by a bunch of impundulu ghosts?*

Yara clapped Darren on the shoulder. "The sooner the better," she said. "It's only a matter of time before Sakura finds a way through our protection spells."

"We'll be in the hall," Ms. Therian said gently. "There's nothing to worry about."

Sefu and Mr. Kimura led Gabriella and Fiona out of the room, and Darren was left alone with the professor. He took a deep breath. *I hope my ancestors are friendly ghosts,* he thought.

The whale's milk, sand, and herb were combined carefully in Mr. Kimura's ivory bowl. The smell tickled Darren's nose, and he had to stifle a laugh when he pictured himself sneezing all over his ghostly ancestors.

Professor Zwane laid two pillows on the floor. He sat cross-legged on one and motioned for Darren to take the other. Then he placed the bowl between them, closed his eyes, and began to chant in a language Darren had never heard before.

A warm glow began to emanate from the bowl. It grew to surround both Darren and the professor. Darren sat bathed in the light for a moment, feeling calm and supported. All his nervousness disappeared. Then he saw people all around him, ethereal and wreathed in light. Men and women were smiling and reaching for him, but nothing about them was frightening. Darren felt reassured in their presence.

The spirits of my ancestors, he thought, *here to protect me.*

Darren wondered if he should thank them but was afraid to break the spell. He closed his eyes and thought the words.

When he reopened them, he saw his ancestors' smiles begin to fade. One by one he watched the joy on their faces turn to worry. And then . . . suddenly nothing. Darren's ancestors disappeared along with the warm glow.

Professor Zwane opened his eyes.

Darren saw concern etched on the professor's face.

Chapter 2
How to Break a Curse

Fiona stood outside of Professor Zwane's office with the others, straining to hear something of what was going on inside. The professor chanted words she couldn't understand in his deep rumble of a voice. Then there was silence and a kind of peaceful glow around the door. After a few moments she heard Darren's voice, but she couldn't catch the words.

Finally, Professor Zwane opened the door, his face unreadable. Darren's expression was clear. He was anxious and upset.

Mr. Kimura broke the silence. "Was there a problem with the spell?" he asked.

The professor nodded, ushering them inside. "Something is blocking his ancestors' magic, and I think I know what it is." He turned to Darren, who was just getting to his feet. "Darren, in case you haven't shared this information with your friends, do you mind if I tell them?"

Tell us what? Fiona wondered as she closed the door behind her and settled in. *It's bad enough that Mack is missing. Is there some kind of terrible secret surrounding Darren, too?*

Darren nodded, but he didn't say a word.

"Darren's family has been living under a curse," the professor said. "An ancient and powerful curse."

"A curse?" Fiona gasped. She couldn't help but notice that that First Four didn't seem at all surprised by that news. "What kind of curse? Is Darren in danger?"

"The Spider's Curse?" Mr. Kimura said knowingly. "It must be. I had my suspicions, especially when I realized Darren had no immediate *impundulu* relatives."

Sefu continued. "But when we saw how great Darren's raw power was, we doubted that a curse could be restraining it."

Ms. Therian turned to Darren with a sense of wonder. "You are so powerful already. When the curse is broken, you will likely feel your power tenfold."

"Sorry to interrupt, but what does that mean?" Fiona asked. "What's the Spider's Curse?" The expressions around her were all so grim, Darren's included, that she was getting really scared.

She noticed that Gabriella was twisting the Ring of Tezcatlipoca around and around on her finger.

She's nervous also, Fiona realized. *We lost Mack. We can't lose Darren to Sakura too.*

Professor Zwane quickly brought Gabriella and Fiona up to speed on the *anansi-impundulu* conflict, and the curse.

"So Darren might have family members right now who are *impundulus*, but they don't know it?" Fiona asked.

"That's certainly possible," Ms. Therian answered. "The curse keeps those abilities from developing. Only Darren's powers were strong enough to manifest, despite the curse, though even now, they are still restrained. But yes, there could be even more *impundulus* in his bloodline. Cousins, aunts—even very distant relatives who Darren isn't aware of."

"I know how much Darren would like that," Fiona said. She smiled at Darren, and he nearly smiled back.

"There's more to it," the professor said. "If Darren wants protection from Sakura with this spell, he'll need to break the curse on his bloodline. His ancestors want to help him, but they can't. The poison prevents them from reaching him."

"If he's able to free the *impundulu* powers of his ancestors, they will be able to offer him the protection he needs," Mr. Kimura confirmed.

Sefu sighed. "We stopped breaking the Spider Curses long ago, after it proved disastrous. Too many Changers were coming into their powers at the same time with no explanations and no one to guide them."

"Think of how scared and freaked out they must have been," Darren said quietly.

Gabriella shuddered. "I remember the first time I noticed that my eyes had turned yellow," she said. "The morning of the first day of school, before Ms. Therian told us what we were. I was so scared. I didn't want to leave my bathroom, but I couldn't exactly tell my mom that my eyes had suddenly turned into cat eyes."

"I saw electric sparks at my fingertips," Darren said. "I could've hurt someone."

"Imagine that happening to a few hundred *impundulu* Changers all at the same time," Sefu said.

He went on to explain that it had been nearly impossible to trace the lineage of everyone connected to the ancient curse. "Many of the cursed *impundulus* were brought to the New World in chains, in the bottoms of slave ships. All records of their ancestors were lost. As the curse on each family was broken, people around the world began to develop their abilities without any kind of help from the Changer network."

"That was especially dangerous for *impundulus*," Yara added. "One flick of the wrist at the wrong time could down a power grid or burn a whole city. Not to mention the panic a bird with an enormous wingspan can cause in the middle of a public square."

"We had to stop efforts to break the curses," Sefu said.

Fiona winced. She could understand the danger in suddenly freeing a mass of *impundulus* without any support, but at the same time, the idea of Changers being purposely kept from their powers made her bristle. A Changer's powers were a part of who he or she was at their very core. Without them, a Changer was incomplete.

These people have to know that something important is missing from their lives, she thought, *even if they can't say exactly what that is.*

Fiona reached into the secret compartment of her backpack and stroked her *selkie* cloak for comfort. She couldn't imagine being without it. Even before she turned twelve and learned she was a *selkie* princess, Fiona longed to be a part of the sea. She grew up beside it. The sound of waves lulled her to sleep every night and comforted her when she was sad. The rhythm of the tides and the waves were as familiar to her as the sound of her father's voice or the beating of her own heart.

What must it be like to be an impundulu *who can never spread his or her wings?* She hated the very idea of that.

Gabriella must have been thinking the same thing. "So it's not bad enough that *impundulus* were enslaved, they had to be denied their powers, too?"

"There is currently a new process in place for breaking the curses," Sefu said. "It requires the *impundulu* in question to put together a complete family tree, stemming from the original *impundulu* who was cursed."

"All of his or her descendants then have to be mapped, tracked down, and monitored when the curse is eventually broken," Ms. Therian said. "My network watches for signs of Changer activity so that we can protect and guide the new Changers."

"That's *if* the cursed person knows he or she is an *impundulu* in the first place," Gabriella said. "Darren's an exception, right?"

Ms. Therian nodded. "Not everyone knows, of course."

"Isn't this an emergency?" Fiona asked. "Does Darren really have to trace his entire family tree? Surely we can skip this step, if that's all it takes?"

Yara shook her head. "I'm afraid it's more complicated than that. Cursed *impundulus* must get forgiveness from the *anansi* bloodline that cursed them. The *anansis* are tricky. I don't think they would allow it, even if we could agree that was the best thing to do. They'll insist that we trace Darren's family, from the first *impundulu* to the present day."

"But my ancestors were slaves," Darren said quietly. "How can I make a family tree if there aren't any records of my relatives from before the Civil War?"

"I can trace some of your roots using magic," Professor Zwane told him. "It can take a long time to form a complete tree, but I think I can do it."

"Time is exactly what we don't have, Sidima," Mr. Kimura said. "Sakura is on the move."

"I'm not teaching any summer classes. If I devote all my attention to it, I think I can do most of the work in a month," Professor Zwane said. "I can call in favors from other influential *impundulus*. The tree won't be complete, but we might have enough information to convince the *anansi* to break the curse."

Mr. Kimura bowed. "I thank you. This is our best hope of protecting Darren."

"I'll do my best, Akira," Professor Zwane said, bowing in return.

Fiona silently wished him luck. *It's not just about protecting Darren, although that is the most important thing,* she thought. *I'd really like him to have Changer family members, too. I know that's important to him.*

Fiona had been alone in her powers too until she found out her mother was a *selkie*. She didn't realize how much she needed her mother's teachings and her guidance until she was thrust into her first *selkie* song lessons. But . . . there was something else Fiona didn't know she needed: companionship, someone who understood her powers in the ways only another *selkie* could.

And Darren hated his powers at first, Fiona remembered. *He was so afraid of hurting someone by accident. I think discovering that his mother or his brother is an* impundulu *would be a huge relief to him. He would have someone to share his feelings with.*

"What about the curse?" Fiona asked. "Tracing his family tree is just part of it, right? Once you do that, how do we help him break the curse?"

Darren, who had been largely silent since the group learned about his curse, was able to answer Fiona's question. "I have to find a descendant of the spider who first cursed my family and convince him or her to grant forgiveness to me and my bloodline."

"There are some *anansi* families who still hold grudges, centuries after the conflict," Professor Zwane explained. "Darren will have to be careful in the way he approaches them."

"Dealings with the *anansis* right now are especially tricky," Sefu added. "They haven't joined Sakura, but they've traditionally been suspicious of the First Four. There hasn't been an *anansi* member of the First Four for a very long time, and that's caused some resentment."

Fiona's head sometimes spun with confusion and dismay over the old rifts among the Changers. The *selkie* faction, for instance, had kept themselves separate from the rest of the Changer world for years.

All this fighting is so dumb. I hope that Darren, Gabriella, Mack, and I can bring about peace as the next First Four. We're in this together, after all.

"How can we find out which *anansi* family cursed mine?" Darren asked.

"I can perform a spell that will reveal from whom you need to seek forgiveness," Professor Zwane said. He rummaged through a cupboard for a minute and then came back with a dried flower on a long stem.

"This is dried *imphepho*, a plant that grows in South Africa," he explained. "It will show us the face of the *anansi* who can break your curse."

"Does everyone need to leave the room again?" Darren asked.

"No, they can stay for this one." The professor placed the dried plant in the now-empty ivory bowl and held a lit match to it.

Fiona breathed in the sharp smell while Professor Zwane chanted in the same ancient language he had used earlier. She sensed a melody in it, but it wasn't the songs of the sea. It was something else she couldn't pinpoint. *Maybe the shifting of the clouds in the sky*, she thought. *Or the rhythm of thunder.*

She watched a circle of glowing blue mist rise from the bowl. The mist shimmered for a moment and looked opaque. Then a face appeared—the face of a beautiful young girl. The mist circled her face like a wreath.

Chapter 3
THE ANANSI PRINCESS

Darren watched the face emerge from the glowing mist. He had been expecting to see a wizened old man, or a grandmother, or someone his mom's age. This girl caught him off guard. She looked to be about twelve or thirteen, just like him.

More than that, she was the kind of girl who often left Darren feeling embarrassed and tongue-tied. *She's pretty,* he thought. He couldn't take his eyes off her. But it wasn't just her looks that threw him off guard; it was the sure confidence in her eyes. *She's not a girl who ever gets tongue-tied,* he thought.

Professor Zwane's voice brought him back to the

office and reality. "That's Esi Akosua," he said.

The blue mist began to dissipate, and along with it, the girl's face. Darren almost wanted to call her back. *Esi Akosua,* he repeated silently to himself. Even her name sounded beautiful.

"That's more bad news, I'm afraid," Sefu said. "Esi is the daughter of one of the *anansi* elders, a man who is arguably their leader. Unfortunately, he's also one of the First Four's most outspoken critics. Getting an apology from her family for a youngling under our protection will be incredibly difficult, if not impossible."

Oh great, Darren thought. *This girl and her dad hate me already. Why can't anything just be easy?*

"Kwame might be stern, but he is a reasonable man," Mr. Kimura said. "I'll reach out to him and try to arrange a meeting. Even the *anansis* have to know that these are extraordinary times. Sakura's reach is already much too far. We have to work together if we're going to defeat her."

Professor Zwane cleared his throat. "Akira, I think it would be best if the family didn't know that the First Four are involved. Let me speak to Esi's father on Darren's behalf."

Darren watched Mr. Kimura catch Ms. Therian's eye. He could tell they were fighting the urge to object to the professor's plan. The First Four felt responsible for Darren's safety. Fiona's and Gabriella's, too. They wouldn't want to trust a meeting this important to anyone else, even someone on their side.

It's going to be hard for them to let go, especially with Mack still missing, Darren thought. *But it sounds like they're going to have to if they want my curse to be broken.*

"Let me speak to Esi's father on Darren's behalf," the professor repeated, more gently this time. "I have a good relationship with him. I'll go to New York City in person and ask the Akosuas to meet with Darren as a favor to me. They may be more likely to help that way."

Mr. Kimura looked like he was about to object, but the professor didn't give him a chance.

"The *anansis'* grievances against the First Four go way back, no matter how misguided they may be," he said. "And Kwame is . . . stubborn. He isn't one to be told the right path; he has to come to a conclusion on his own."

Darren watched as Ms. Therian, Sefu, and Yara each gave Mr. Kimura a slight nod. They were obviously reluctant to accept the situation, but in the end they had to agree to the wisdom of Professor Zwane's plan.

Mr. Kimura bowed to the professor again. "I thank you, Sidima. I know you'll do your best for Darren."

"You can count on me, Akira," the professor answered.

"Now, let's discuss how best to approach Esi's father and what our next steps should be," Yara said. "We want to be ready to invoke the protection of Darren's ancestors from the very moment the curse is lifted."

"You mean *if* it's lifted, don't you?" Darren asked. "Don't we have to plan for that, too?" He was starting to feel a little overwhelmed. At first he was surprised and scared that they were going to do the protection spell today, and then it hadn't even worked.

And now I find out that the one Changer who can break the spell—a pretty, sophisticated New York City girl—belongs to a family that hates the First Four. What more can go wrong?

The adults picked up on Darren's uneasiness.

"Let's not worry about that yet," Sefu said. "Best to stay positive."

Darren nearly snorted at that. Sefu was always the one preparing for the worst.

"Why don't you kids head downstairs for a while?" Ms. Therian asked. "You're protected here on campus. Go and have some fun exploring while the campus is empty. Forget about all this for a little while. We'll come get you when we're ready to return to Willow Cove."

Darren thought that was probably code for "stop worrying and let the grown-ups figure stuff out now," but he was glad to get out of the office. His mind was still full of the images of his ancestors reaching for him and the way their smiles turned to worry when they were suddenly cut off. And, of course, he kept picturing the *anansi* girl who might be able to save him from the curse and Sakura.

Professor Zwane caught Darren's eye and winked as the three kids filed out. "It'll work out," he said. "Don't worry. Everything's going to be fine."

Is it really going to be fine? Darren wondered. He didn't share the professor's confidence. *If we waste all this time trying to get rid of my curse, by the time we find Mack it might be too late. And if this Esi girl refuses to forgive me, isn't it only a matter of time before Sakura turns me into one of her minions, too?*

Fiona and Gabriella led him out the hallway and downstairs. He wasn't surprised to find that Fiona was heading toward the school's library. She had fallen in love with it on their first visit to Wyndemere Academy in the spring. They had learned some valuable information about Sakura in one of the books there.

"Maybe we'll find a book about *anansi* curses. Something the professor overlooked," Fiona said.

"Unlikely," Darren told her. "Professor Zwane is, like, *the* expert on West and South African tribal myths."

"It never hurts to look," Fiona said.

But on the way to the library they had to walk past the art studio—the room at Wyndemere Academy that had most appealed to Mack. Darren could almost see his friend sitting at a drafting table under the enormous windows, drawing a superhero for one of his many comic books. The image hit Darren so hard that he was breathless for a moment.

Gabriella must have been thinking the same thing. "It's hard to believe that the last time we were here was before Mack—" Her voice caught in her throat.

"You know it wasn't your fault," Fiona said gently.

Darren knew that Gabriella felt guilty about Mack. Very powerful *nahuals*, like Gabriella, had the ability to spirit-walk in other people's minds. Her aunt and grand-mother had done everything they could to teach her to master the skill—a skill that took most *nahuals* decades to perfect—in just one week.

Gabriella had tried, in that last battle with Sakura, to use what she had learned to turn Mack around, but Sakura's hooks were already too deep into him. All of Mack's happiness—his joy, his hope, his love—slowly turned to despair and anger under the Shadow Fox's dark magic. Gabriella tried to get Mack to fight against the desolation, but he couldn't. He discovered what Gabriella was doing and used defensive magic to push her out of his mind.

"You keep saying it's not my fault," Gabriella said, "but—"

"But nothing," Fiona said, cutting her off. "You did your best. We all did our best. Blaming yourself won't help Mack now. Getting him back will. We're going to do that, and before Sakura can do any more damage to him. I know we will."

Darren nodded, but he didn't really share Fiona's confidence, at least not with this curse still hanging over him and his family.

"We'll be together again soon—all four of us," he said.

"I have an idea! Let's make that happen now," Fiona said.

"How?" Gabriella and Darren asked at the same time.

"Let's make a comic book that brings us all together— in honor of Mack," she suggested.

Gabriella's expression brightened a bit. "We can show it to him when he gets back," she said. "So he'll know we didn't give up on him."

"Exactly. Only you have to draw it," Fiona said with a giggle. "I can write the best research paper you've ever seen, but I can only draw stick figures."

The three friends headed into the studio and pulled sketch pads and pencils from the supply closet. Gabriella set to the task, drawing the *nahual* superhero Mack had helped her create a while back, along with a wise *selkie*, a fierce and determined *impundulu*, and the *kitsune* who brought them all together to fight magical crime.

Darren and Fiona made story suggestions and

colored in panels as Gabriella created them.

The three of them chatted quietly, intent on their story.

"I'm sorry about the curse," Fiona said to Darren. "It must have been really upsetting to learn about. Is that why you didn't tell us?"

"Between finals and Changer stuff and Mack's disappearance, there wasn't really time to think about it, let alone tell all of you," Darren said.

"It's kind of exciting to think that someone else in your family might be an *impundulu*," Fiona said, choosing blue, green, and gray pencils to get the colors of the ocean waves just right.

"Yes and no. I guess I have mixed feelings," Darren admitted.

"Why?" Fiona asked.

"I mean, on the one hand, if my mom or dad or Ray is a Changer, I'd be thrilled. It'd be great to feel less alone in my family, to have someone who understands what I've been going through. Plus, I'm not a very good liar, and it's rough having to fib constantly about where I'm going when I'm doing Changer stuff."

Fiona nodded thoughtfully. "My dad knows I'm a *selkie*, and that makes everything easier. But I don't tell him anything about our battles. He'd totally freak and lock me in my room forever. I'm grateful I have my mom to talk things over with."

"But there's a downside to having Changer family too," Gabriella said. "Especially now when we're about to go to war."

"Yeah," Darren agreed, inking in a lightning bolt that stretched across two pages. "But it's not just that. You remember the trouble I had learning to control my powers? I almost fried Fiona in class that first month of school."

Fiona shook her head. Darren noticed that when she did, her long hair gave off the scent of the sea.

"I wasn't hurt," she insisted.

"I almost electrocuted you," Darren said. "But it's not just that. Everything about my life changed after I found out . . . *everything*. I can't hang out with my friends the way I used to, and every time we turn around we're doing battle with someone or something. I'm not sure I would wish that on anyone. If only there was a way to give people a choice, you know? To ask Ray or Mom whether having Changer magic is something they would want."

"Sometimes I wonder if my little sister, Maritza, will have the ability and if I would be more relieved for me or worried for her," Gabriella said. "I just hope we manage to defeat Sakura before she comes of age."

"At least Maritza or Ray wouldn't have to go it alone. You'd be there for them," Fiona pointed out. "That would make everything easier."

"With the divorce stuff finally wrapping up in my family, things are just getting back to a new kind of normal. It's not such a great time for any of them to suddenly develop magical shape-shifting powers."

"How's the divorce going anyway?" Gabriella asked.

"Okay, I guess. It's almost finalized. My parents are sad about it, but they both say it's for the best. Maybe they're right. At least they're not fighting all the time anymore. Not having to listen to that is a relief, at least," Darren said.

"Is the custody all worked out?" Fiona asked gently.

"Last month I went to a therapist the court

recommended and told her who I wanted to live with—my mom. My dad doesn't have a problem with that as long as I see him on weekends. There's a court date next month, but since they already agreed on the terms, it's just a formality."

"That's good," Gabriella said. "It must help to know it'll be over soon."

"It's gone pretty smoothly," Darren continued. "I don't want anything—magical or not—messing it up. At least with all the Changer-related chaos going on, I haven't had to think about that too much either."

Fiona frowned. "Nothing like a power-hungry *kitsune* to put things in perspective," she said darkly.

Darren added the last page, now fully colored in, to their comic book. He and Fiona stood on either side of Gabriella while she flipped through the pages for them.

It was the story of four young Changers—a powerful *kitsune*, a fierce *impundulu*, an agile *nahual*, and a wise *selkie*—who came together to battle evil. And won. The next-to-last spread showed a Shadow Fox and her army giving up in defeat, the four young Changers standing victorious together.

"Will it ever be like this again?" Gabriella asked. "Will the four of us be together?"

Fiona gave her friend's shoulder a squeeze. "It will be," she said. "I know Mack will come back to us."

"And when he does," Darren added, "we'll show this comic book to him. He'll know how much we missed him and how hard we fought to get him back."

Gabriella nodded and wiped her eyes as she turned to the book's final spread. It was a picture of the four of them standing in a circle looking proud and happy.

I *wonder where Mack is now*, Darren thought. *And if any part of him still thinks about the friends he left behind.*

Chapter 4
Sakura's Apprentice

You need to get it right this time, Mack thought. He hated to think of what Sakura would do if he failed again. He didn't want to face her disdain and disappointment.

Get it right! he commanded himself. *You need this. Don't make Sakura think she made a mistake in choosing you to be her apprentice.*

Mack stared at himself in the mirror and willed himself to disappear. He chanted a spell, and a thick mist washed over him. First it erased his feet and ankles. Then it slowly moved up, erasing his legs and most of his torso. He concentrated on making his chest and his shoulders disappear and then continued to his face. The mist was about to cover his eyebrows.

I'm too slow, but it's working, he thought. *Finally!*

But Mack's relief was premature. As soon as he had the thought, as soon as he felt the smallest bit of pride in himself, the mist disappeared. His cloaking illusion had failed. *Again.*

Mack threw himself down onto the tattered couch behind him with a massive sigh. The whole thing creaked, and it had a nasty, musty smell. He kicked the ratty armrest and watched dust motes float in the dim light. He was tired of staying in dusty old holes in the wall.

Sakura should be living in a palace, not this tumbledown shack. I'm going to make sure our army has every luxury as soon as we defeat the First Four.

He was also tired of relocating from base to base. As soon as he felt like they had settled in, Sakura pulled up the stakes again. They moved at least every other week, if not more often. Mack couldn't even remember how many places he had called home since leaving Willow Cove.

That's a lot of new homes for a kid who never lived

anywhere else but that stupid little town. First with my parents, and then—when they died—with the old man.

Mack almost used the familiar "Jiichan," but quickly pushed the Japanese pet name for "grandfather" away. *The old man,* he repeated to himself. *The one who tried to control your power. To block what Sakura can help you become.*

Mack never knew exactly where he was anymore. He didn't know what day it was or what time. They stayed in the dark most hours of the day, and he had long since gotten rid of his cell phone so that the First Four couldn't use human technology to track him. Sakura's cloaking spells blocked them from finding him using magic.

They weren't exactly living in the lap of luxury, but that wasn't important. Luxury would come after victory. What mattered was staying out of the hands of the First Four until he and Sakura were powerful enough to defeat them.

Sakura was helping him do exactly that. Her methods were a lot rougher than Ms. Therian's had been, but Mack knew it would be worth it in the end. Worth it when he gained another tail, and another, and another.

He planned to earn all nine—the highest number a *kitsune* could achieve.

I'm no weakling who needs to be coddled by the First Four, he told himself. *I can handle whatever Sakura tests me with. I have to.*

"You're running out of time, apprentice," said a voice.

Mack scrambled to his feet. Sakura materialized in front of him. She had crept up on him using the exact same cloaking illusion that Mack had failed to perfect.

"Master," Mack said with a deep bow. "I'm working my hardest. I'll get it soon; I just need a few more days—"

"You've had *weeks*," Sakura sneered. "It's crucial that you master the illusion for the next steps in our plan. I won't fail because *you're* too weak to learn a simple spell."

"I'm very close," Mack said. "I'm almost there. I promise. Don't give up on me."

Sakura scoffed at him. "*Close* is not good enough. You need to learn a lot more than that simple cloaking spell. I need you to be able to alter your appearance, as well." She stepped closer and stared down at Mack's bowed head, looking at him as if he were garbage. "Did I make a mistake in choosing you as my apprentice? Should I turn you over to your little friends from Willow Cove? Is that where you belong?"

"No! They're weak. I'm strong, like you. I'll get the spell—and more. I just need a little more time," he pleaded. "Don't send me away."

"Perhaps it's time to up the ante." Sakura snapped her fingers. Adam, a *nykur*—an Icelandic horse Changer who could control water—appeared.

"Master," Adam said. "What do you command?"

"I want you to hunt Mack until he's able to master the cloaking illusion. Don't let up until he's successful." She swept out of the room.

Mack and Adam both bowed to her retreating form. "Yes, Master," they said in unison.

Sakura didn't wait for their answers. She never did. She knew her orders would be followed. No one dared disobey her.

Adam smirked at Mack. "No special treatment now, *boy*," he drawled.

The words were still hanging in the air when he transformed and jumped at Mack.

Mack transformed too. *Kitsunes* had the advantage

of speed, but as he'd learned at Wyndemere Academy (which seemed like a lifetime ago), *nykurs* were not to be underestimated. Luckily, he'd gotten a crash course in evasive maneuvers from a professor there that put him at a slight advantage.

Mack twisted just out of reach of the *nykur* and ran downstairs into the entry hall of the broken-down Victorian mansion. Shadowy flames licked at his paws, charring the hardwood floor beneath him. These flames were dark with a mysterious power, unlike the bright orange and yellow flames he had sported when he first became a *kitsune*. His fur was different now too. Instead of the bright pure white it had been, it was more muted now, with strands of charcoal and gray.

Mack hoped that the more he learned, the more he mastered, and the more powerful his dark flames would become. Sakura's *kitsune* flames absorbed light and turned it into darkness. Mack wanted to do the same.

He threw himself around a corner, but Adam was gaining on him.

He's had it in for me since day one, Mack thought. *They all have.*

Most of Sakura's forces made no secret of their contempt for her newest apprentice.

The First Four and the rest of Mack's old friends had been fighting and imprisoning Sakura's forces nonstop since Mack joined them, but that wasn't Mack's fault. He didn't know why the old man and his cronies kept hunting for him. He had made his choice. He wouldn't unmake it.

Adam and the others blame me for my grandfather, he thought. *Don't they know I turned my back on the old man and the rest of the First Four when I joined Sakura? I'm one of them now.*

The special treatment Sakura gave her new apprentice earned Mack even more enemies. Mack was clearly her favorite, and the rest of her soldiers were just plain jealous.

No matter, Mack thought. *When I learn all I have to learn from Sakura, I'll be her highest-ranking general. Then they'll have to do what I say. And bow down to me. I'll make sure Adam gets what's coming to him.*

Mack's mind was so full of his vision of revenge that he nearly forgot the *nykur* was still chasing him. He had run upstairs and down. He even found what looked like a secret staircase, but Adam was never far behind. Now Mack heard the thundering of hooves right behind him. Adam was gaining again, and fast.

Mack skidded to a stop behind an old, sheet-covered armoire. Hidden, he recited the cloaking spell again, concentrating harder than he had ever concentrated in his life. He watched his paws fade away, but his focus was broken when Adam galloped into the room. The *nykur* kicked over the armoire, leaving Mack out in the open.

Mack jumped out of the way just in time to avoid a drenching as the *nykur* conjured a raging river. Mack bounded down a flight of stairs to the first floor, turned at the bottom, and threw fireballs back at Adam, who easily used his water abilities to put out the flames. Steam rose from the steps.

Mack was exhausted from running and fighting. He was down to the last of his energy. Any minute now Adam was going to catch him and give him the beating of his life. And Mack knew the *nykur* would enjoy that more than anything.

All of Sakura's soldiers will love that, Mack thought. *They'll gather around to watch. They'll laugh. They'll jeer. They'll say I had it coming.*

It was as if Adam could read Mack's mind. The *nykur* whinnied and spoke to Mack telepathically—the only way Changers could communicate in their animal forms.

It's just a matter of time, boy. Where are you?

Fury coursed through Mack. Dark flames burst from his paws. *It's not fair!*

Adam snickered again, fueling Mack's anger and frustration.

Rage gave Mack the determination he needed. He turned a corner into an old dining room and chanted the cloaking illusion spell once again. This time it was perfect. Just as Adam entered the room, Mack disappeared.

Right in front of his eyes! Mack cheered silently to himself.

Now Adam was the angry one while Mack held back a laugh so he wouldn't give his position away.

Now who's going to be a laughingstock? Mack thought.

The *nykur* howled. He started bucking and over-turning chairs—even the dusty old dining table—as he searched for his mark.

Mack danced around him and then padded quietly back upstairs to his room. He collapsed on the tattered old sofa, still invisible.

This feeling—joy at the humiliation of someone else—was the closest thing Mack had felt to happiness since he joined Sakura. He wanted more of this. Especially when he realized his master had noticed and approved.

Very good, apprentice, Sakura communicated telepathically to him. *You'll have a new tail in no time. And soon—soon—the world will be ours.*

Chapter 5
ESI AKOSUA

Darren nervously checked the mirror and straightened his collar for the tenth time that morning. He was wearing a button-down shirt and one of Ray's ties. He also wore his best pants and had polished his dress shoes to a high shine. He even spritzed on a bit of the cologne his father had given him for Christmas.

He was just waiting for Professor Zwane to arrive. The two of them were headed to New York City today to meet Esi Akosua and ask for her help.

By this time tomorrow the curse might be lifted. Then my ancestors will be able to protect me from Sakura, and the rest of us can go back to searching for Mack again, Darren thought.

He tried not to think about the fact that some of his family members might also develop *impundulu* powers.

But first he had to make a good impression on Esi and her father.

Darren had checked all the social media sites looking for more information about Esi and her family before the meeting, but he found nothing. It was as if the girl didn't even exist in the modern world, at least not under her own name.

"Esi's father will be at the meeting too," Professor Zwane had said when he called the day before. "And don't be surprised if she's surrounded by bodyguards. She and her father are the closest thing the Changer world has to *anansi* royalty. They're protected at all times, especially now that Sakura's on the move."

He went on to explain that Esi and her family knew nothing about Darren's special relationship with the current First Four.

"I haven't even told them that you're from Willow Cove," he had said. "That would surely tip them off."

"What did you tell them?" Darren asked.

"Only that I met you when you visited Wyndemere

Academy and that I identified the curse when you sat in on one of my classes," he answered.

Darren knew how essential it was to keep his real identity a secret. For some reason the *anansi* didn't trust the First Four.

If Esi and her family find out I'm tied to Mr. Kimura and the others, they'll refuse to forgive my bloodline, and I'll have to live under the curse forever, Darren thought. *Considering how long Changers live, that could be hundreds of years. Not to mention I'll be a sitting duck for Sakura.*

As far as Darren knew, the *anansi* hadn't joined Sakura's evil army, but he had to acknowledge that that was a possibility, too. That they already knew all about Darren, and they intended to capture him and hand him over to the Shadow Fox immediately as a token of loyalty.

It's possible that Professor Zwane and I are walking into a trap—or in this case, a sticky spiderweb.

Darren took one last look in the mirror just as Ray walked by. Darren's mom and brother believed that he was going on a visit to Wyndemere Academy to look at the school and meet with professors.

"Don't worry, bro," Ray said with a teasing tone. "The boarding school girls are going to love you."

"I don't care about them," Darren snapped. Snapping at Ray wasn't like him, but the truth was that his big brother had come a little too close to the truth. Darren cared very much what Esi Akosua thought of him. His life could very well depend on that.

"Whoa!" Ray said, holding his hands up in surrender. "I'm just kidding."

Darren shook his head. "I know. Sorry. I guess I'm just a little nervous." Then he grinned. "As long as you're not with me, at least the girls won't run away in horror."

Ray laughed and then got more serious. "The school—girls and all—is going to love you. Just be yourself."

"I will," Darren said. He affected a swagger as he walked toward the stairs. "And I'll try not to make all the girls fall in love with me."

Ray laughed again. "Go on, Romeo. Have fun."

Darren found his mother to say good-bye. His mom was superproud of Darren for being selected to visit an elite boarding school, especially given the upset surrounding his parents' divorce.

Maybe she's an impundulu *too,* he thought. *By this time tomorrow I might be able to tell her the truth about where I'm really going and what I'm doing when I disappear like this.* He almost laughed at the idea of his mom's reaction to traveling by *tengu. She never even drives above the speed limit.*

"See you tonight," Darren called over his shoulder, and headed outside.

"Have fun!" his mother responded. "Take lots of pictures! And don't forget—we need application deadlines and information about tuition. Just bring me a packet!"

Professor Zwane, Fiona, and Gabriella waited for him by the professor's car. The First Four couldn't join them, of course, but Fiona and Gabriella could still move around anonymously. The rest of the Changer world didn't know about the prophecy yet, although there were lots of rumors—especially because the four of them had defeated the evil warlock Auden Ironbound.

The girls wouldn't risk discovery by coming to Darren's meeting with Esi and her father, but they would be nearby in case there was trouble with Sakura or with the *anansi.* He was glad to know his friends would be ready to jump in and fight if they were needed.

Darren wasn't surprised to find Margaery waiting in the driver's seat of the car.

"It's been a really, really long time since I've driven," Margaery said, stepping on the gas while the car was still in park.

"Margaery, I think you need to put it in drive," Professor Zwane said. "Otherwise, you're just revving the engine."

"Oh, right," she said sheepishly.

Margaery drove, a little unsteadily, around the corner and stopped. She looked visibly calmer when she put the car in park and closed her eyes. Darren felt the usual stillness come over them and then a *whoosh*. He had never been in a vehicle for a wind transport before.

Can she really move a car? he wondered. *Is her magic over the wind strong enough to carry a two-ton vehicle all the way across the country?*

Darren's question was answered when the car settled gently in the middle of a parking lot. Instead of the quiet from a moment before, Darren heard horns honking, sirens blaring, and a taxi driver yelling at a pedestrian.

Darren had never been to New York City before, but it sounded just as loud and chaotic as it did in the movies.

"I guess we're here," he said.

Margaery nodded and then chanted a quick spell under her breath. The parking attendant who had been staring at them stunned and openmouthed went back inside his little booth, as if a car with five people inside hadn't just dropped out of the sky and landed quietly between an SUV and a Volkswagen Beetle.

The five of them headed out of the lot and started to walk down Broadway. Darren was too nervous to notice the flashing billboards, the souvenir shops, and the theaters advertising plays and musicals. In a few minutes he'd meet Esi Akosua and her father and place his future and maybe even his life in their hands.

Professor Zwane turned down a side street and pointed to a Brazilian restaurant where they would meet Esi and her father for lunch.

"We'll wait in there," Margaery said, pointing to a souvenir shop just across the street. "We'll be on high alert, ready to intervene if something goes wrong."

Darren and the professor held back and watched Margaery, Fiona, and Gabriella walk down the street and into the shop like any other tourists. They didn't want anyone in the restaurant to see that the professor and Darren had other companions.

Professor Zwane turned to Darren. "Ready?" he asked.

Darren took a deep breath and checked to make sure his shirt was neatly tucked in. "Let's go," he answered, wiping his sweaty palms on his pants.

They stepped into the cool, dark restaurant, and Darren immediately felt underdressed, like a kid playing at dress up. The place was full of big, serious-looking men and women in dark suits. They all wore ties.

Two of the suits came forward and wordlessly led Darren and the professor toward a booth in the restaurant's back corner.

They must be the bodyguards, Darren thought. Then he caught sight of Esi, nestled in the booth. Her yellow sundress was a spot of sunshine in the middle of the dark restaurant. *She's even prettier than she was in Professor Zwane's spell*, he thought.

A big bear of a man sat next to her wearing another one of those dark suits. As they neared, the man stood. Professor Zwane was a tall man, but Esi's father seemed to tower over him.

"Kwame," Professor Zwane said to him with a bow.

"Sidima," Esi's father answered with a slight nod.

The professor waved Darren into the booth. He slid onto the bench and found himself sitting directly across from Esi. She eyed him curiously while the professor took the seat across from her father.

Darren relaxed a little when Esi smiled at him. Then she turned her eyes toward Professor Zwane and listened carefully while he explained his discovery of the curse.

"We know that Sakura is targeting the vulnerable," the professor explained, "younglings as well as adults. Darren doesn't have any family members to protect him. With Sakura's forces on the move, I tried to cast a protection spell to ensure his safety from her memory eating. But the spell is blocked by the curse. His ancestors can't break through."

Esi's father eyed Darren up and down. Darren couldn't help but feel judged.

He felt like a little kid. *I should have asked Mom to buy me a suit jacket,* he thought. *Ray would have thought of that.*

Finally Esi's father spoke. "The children of *anansis* hold nothing against the *impundulus* any longer. We're always willing to break old curses when we can," he said, "but I am troubled by one thing."

Darren took a deep breath.

"What is it?" Professor Zwane asked.

Esi's father's serious eyes bored into the professor's. "I've heard rumors about a young *impundulu,* a friend of Akira Kimura's grandson. Interesting rumors."

Darren swallowed and tried not to let his face show how intimidated he was.

Whether Mr. Akosua noticed or not, he continued, narrowing his eyes. "I've also heard that they—along with two more younglings—are being trained by Dorina Therian. Do you also know of these rumors, old friend?"

Professor Zwane's eyes widened, but he kept his expression neutral. He opened his mouth to respond. Only he didn't, because at that very second there was a giant crash.

Darren looked over his shoulder and saw that a *nykur*, a phoenix, and an *impundulu* had burst through the restaurant's front window. There was a swarm of other Changers at their backs.

Darren recognized them as Sakura's forces. Many of them had taken part in the battle that ended with Mack going over to Sakura.

The *anansi* bodyguards immediately transformed and jumped into battle mode. They were *huge* spiders—and terrifying.

Darren signaled to Esi, and the two of them dove under the table. The professor and Esi's father moved to fight alongside the guards.

"They're after me!" he shouted to Esi.

At the same time Esi shouted, "They're after me!"

"They're after you?" they asked each other in unison.

An entire wall of glass behind the two of them shattered.

"We need to get out of here," Darren yelled over the uproar. "I have to get the two of us to safety."

"No, I have to get the two of us to safety," Esi snapped.

She motioned to a door. They ran toward it. A

phoenix spotted them and gave chase, but Darren threw lightning bolts to slow it down. At the same time Esi blew a choking cloud of murky mist behind them.

Miasma, Darren realized. *Professor Zwane once mentioned that* anansis *have the power to release an airborne poison that can stun their opponent.*

Darren held his breath as the two of them dashed through the kitchen and out the restaurant's back door into an alley. Darren's first thought was to change into his *impundulu* form and fly to safety. He wasn't sure his wings were strong enough to carry Esi as a human, but perhaps he could carry her as a spider. . . .

"Exactly how big are you when you transform?" he asked, scanning the alley.

"Excuse me?" Esi asked with a withering look. "We're in danger and you want to know how *big* I am?"

"Are you a tiny spider or, like, a giant spider?" Darren asked frantically.

"Giant," Esi said proudly.

"Then flying out of here won't work," Darren said. "I don't think I can fly with a giant spider, or even a human girl, on my back. I wouldn't want to risk it anyway."

He ran to the end of the alley and cautiously peeked across the street. There was no sign of Fiona, Gabriella, and Margaery in the window of the souvenir shop.

They must have joined the fight, Darren thought. *I should be with them.*

Then he remembered his lack of protection and realized that was a terrible idea. *If Sakura shows up, they can resist her mind control. I can't. I'd better do what the First Four always told me to do: get to safety and wait for help to arrive.*

He ran back to Esi. "We have to get out of here until the coast is clear. Any ideas?"

"Shouldn't we stay and fight?" Esi asked. "Or are you afraid?"

"I'm not afraid. But if we're the targets, it's too dangerous to stay. And dangerous for our friends, too," Darren said. "Let's get somewhere safe and then check in with the group."

"I can't just leave," Esi told him. "My father's inside."

Just as she turned to go back in through the kitchen door, a massive explosion ripped through the restaurant.

Going back wasn't an option anymore.

"Your father would want you to get somewhere safe,"

Darren said, pulling her down the alley. "We'll check in with him and the professor as soon as we can."

Reluctantly, Esi agreed.

"Any ideas?" Darren asked. "You live here, right?"

"Pssh. I live in Westchester."

"And that is in . . . ?"

"It's more than an hour north, and the next train doesn't leave for another forty-five minutes."

"Anyplace closer, then?"

"I have a cousin who lives a few subway stops from here," she suggested.

"Okay, that'll have to do."

Together they ran a few blocks on Broadway. Then Esi led him down a flight of stairs to the New York City subway.

I hope Sakura can't find us down here, Darren thought. *If she does, we'll be trapped underground.*

Chapter 6
A FIGHT AMONG FRIENDS

Mack arrived at the steakhouse at the back of Sakura's forces, frustrated that Sakura wouldn't allow him to be in the lead. They had good information that some of those who were loyal to the First Four would be inside—including Darren—asking the *anansis* for help of some kind. How typical of him. Asking for help, when he could test his power instead. Mack knew that meant that Fiona and Gabriella wouldn't be far away.

Those kids are always together, he thought with a sneer. *It's like the First Four brainwashed them to stick together. And even if they manage to escape, Sakura said there's a relic to capture,* Mack remembered. *Not to mention the fact that a* brutal *show of strength will finally force the* anansis *to join the right side of the fight—our side.*

Chaos reigned all around. Sakura's forces battled those of the First Four and the *anansis*. But Mack only had eyes for the booth in the back. Sakura had told him that's where he would find Darren and Esi—each one alone would be a huge prize. Mack intended to capture them both. He couldn't wait to see the look on Sakura's face when he dropped them both at her feet.

She'll never question her decision to make me an apprentice again. I wouldn't be surprised if I leave here with a fourth tail.

But the booth was empty. Mack cast around for them with his mind, but he sensed they were both gone, along with the girl's father, the *anansi* leader. His anger and frustration erupted in a burst of shadowy flame. *I'm too late!*

Then he heard a familiar voice. Fiona was speaking to him telepathically.

Mack, we're here. It's us, she said.

He spun on his heel. Fiona was right behind him, wearing her *selkie* cloak, singing a *selkie* song.

Mack didn't answer. The fireballs he shot in her direction were answer enough, but Fiona quickly spun a wall of water around herself to douse them.

In a rage he shot fireball after fireball, but each one simply turned to steam when they met the water.

You're coming back with us, Mack, Fiona said. *Back where you belong.*

Mack threw his head back and laughed. Fiona might be able to douse a fireball or two, but the idea of a *weakling* like her taking on a *power* like Mack was ridiculous, even before he'd had all of Sakura's special training.

I am where I belong, Mack said, circling her. *Don't even try to capture me. I'll knock you out before you can even begin another one of your silly protection songs.*

To prove that, he took a step forward, ready to take her on one-on-one. He'd create a round of fireballs so big and powerful that her wall of water would evaporate, and then he'd capture her just like the First Four were capturing Sakura's people.

He raised a paw, but before he could work his magic, a strange feeling came over him.

What's happening to me? he wondered.

Warm, joyful memories surged through him. He remembered laughing with Fiona, Gabriella, and Darren over pizza. He remembered teaching Gabriella how to draw a comic; riding his bike with his best friend, Joel; and even confiding some of his hopes for the future in Darren while they practiced shooting fire arrows at a moving target.

This is happiness, he realized. *I feel happy.*

Mack saw that his dark flames were flickering. They sputtered, and then they went out completely. He lost his grip on his *kitsune* form and changed back to a human, stumbling backward and banging into an overturned chair. He ended up on his back on the floor while magic exploded all around him. Fiona stood over him.

"That's it, Mack. It's working. Embrace your good memories and come back to us!" she urged. "We miss you. We need you."

I'm on the wrong side of this fight, Mack thought. *How did I get here? Where's my grandfather? Where's Jiichan?*

He was about to ask Fiona when he heard another voice. Someone else was communicating to him. It was the master's voice.

Apprentice! You're being weak. Find the nahual. She's manipulating you.

Weak? In a flash Mack jumped to his feet. Anger flooded through him again along with all the pain he had been carrying inside since he joined Sakura. The anger and pain that made him who he was. The anger and pain that made him powerful. He transformed back into a *kitsune*, and the dark flames ignited again.

"No!" Fiona cried. "Fight it, Mack! Fight it!"

Mack smirked as she began to sing, drawing the water around her again and trying to extinguish his dark flames. He quickly sidestepped her, his flames growing bigger and darker.

Not today, selkie, he thought.

Mack cast around with his mind again, except now he was looking for the *nahual's* spirit while he readied another attack. *She's well-hidden in my thoughts and memories,* he realized. *I'll have to attack her physical form to get rid of her.*

He shot a burst of fire arrows at Fiona, piercing her wall of water.

"No!" Fiona yelled. She seemed to be trying to signal someone.

Mack followed her gaze and directed a barrage of

arrows at the restaurant's dessert case. He incinerated the back of the wooden case in an instant, revealing Gabriella. The *nahual* was sitting cross-legged, meditating, and she was still spirit-walking in Mack's mind.

Get out! Mack communicated to her.

She shook her head, her eyes still closed.

How dare she? he thought. He readied another fire arrow. *Your turn to fry, nahual!*

At that moment Gabriella transformed into her *nahual* form and leaped out of his way. But at least he had succeeded in ejecting her from his mind. Mack's arrow hit a mirror, shattering it and the glass plates behind the case. While the desserts burned, Fiona and Gabriella moved toward each other. Fiona's wall of water surrounded the *nahual*, too, protecting them both from Mack's fire.

A *tengu* was using her wings to create wind gusts, ones that Sakura's forces were struggling against. Mack recognized her—she was Margaery, the bird who worked for the First Four. A man, an *impundulu* Mack had never seen before, was helping her, too.

Sakura's army pushed against the wind. They were

moving in on the *tengu* and *impundulu*, despite the wind gusts, when Mack saw Fiona and Gabriella dart toward the birds. If they reached Margaery, all four of them could escape. Mack and the others would have to return to Sakura empty-handed.

"No!" Mack howled. He hurled a burst of flame at the small group and communicated to Sakura's people. *Don't let them get to the* tengu! *Stop them!*

But it was too late. Just as he finished his sentence, the two Willow Cove younglings, the *tengu*, and the *impundulu* collided and disappeared in a gust of wind.

Mack sent an angry barrage of fire across the room, nearly burning Adam in the process.

He let out an angry howl. Not only had they let their prime targets—Darren and Esi—escape, he had also wasted a chance to catch the other two members of the next First Four.

Sakura won't be pleased. I have to find a way to turn this around. I need a prize to show the master. Or else.

Chapter 7
SPIDER GIRL

Darren followed Esi down the stairs to the New York City subway system. Esi stopped at a machine to buy a Metrocard that would let them through the turnstiles and onto the train. Darren pulled out his wallet and tried to mirror her movements at the machine next to hers, but she waved him off.

"There's no time," she said. "And quit looking so nervous. The police will stop you for looking suspicious."

Darren tried to relax while he watched Esi slide a credit card into a slot and punch buttons like an expert. A second later a yellow-and-black card popped out of the machine. He trailed her as she rushed hastily through a turnstile, but it wouldn't let him through.

"You need to swipe the card before you can go through," she commanded, handing the Metrocard to him over the turnstile.

Darren did as he was told, but still no dice.

"Slower," she said, exasperated.

Darren made a conscious effort to slow down, and the turnstile finally admitted him. Then Esi turned on her heel, and Darren had to struggle to keep up with her long, confident strides. He followed her through one tunnel and then another. They wove in and out of groups of rushing New Yorkers and slower-moving tourists.

Finally, they ran down another flight of stairs and found themselves on a subway platform. A train pulled into the station, the doors opened, and they got on. Darren didn't feel safe until the doors closed behind them. The car they were in was mostly empty.

He took a deep breath and then pulled out his phone. "I'll check in with my friends," he said.

"Don't bother," Esi told him. "You won't get great service underground."

Darren shoved the phone back into his pocket,

blushing. *I guess I should have known that,* he thought.

He leaned closer to Esi and whispered, "So . . . why is Sakura after you?"

"Isn't it obvious?" Esi asked. "Sakura needs the *anansis* if she has any shot of winning this war. So she's trying to force us to join her. My father's been suspecting a kidnapping for months now. Sakura will hold me hostage to demand their support."

Darren tried to ignore the superior tone of her statement, but his cheeks turned even redder. Still, he needed a fuller picture of what was really going on. Was Sakura really after Esi? Or had her followers come to the restaurant to kidnap him? Or both?

"But I thought the *anansis* were already thinking of siding with her against the First Four," Darren said. "Why would your father be worried about a kidnapping by a potential ally?"

"Typical," Esi snorted. "You don't know anything about the *anansis*. If you did, then you'd know that my father rejected Sakura's deal months ago. That didn't stop other *anansi* families from going over to her side, but my father and his closest followers didn't."

Darren felt confused. "Some *anansis* joined her army even though your father—their leader—rejected Sakura's deal?" he asked.

"*Anansis* aren't like the *selkies*," she said disdainfully. "We're not a uniform group that follows one leader like the *selkie* faction does. *Anansis* have minds of their own. And we use them. Why can't any of the other Changers wrap their brains around that?"

I have a lot to learn about anansis, Darren thought. *But Esi has a lot to learn about other Changers, too. The First Four's supporters aren't blind followers. And selkies do have minds of their own. You only have to spend five minutes with Fiona to know that.*

Even so, now was not the time to school Esi on the ways of the First Four or the *selkies*. Sakura's soldiers could be right on their heels.

"If Sakura has other *anansis* on her side, why does she need your family in particular?" he asked. He didn't say it, but if *anansis* had minds of their own, it didn't sound like kidnapping Esi would affect anyone other than her father.

Now it was Esi's turn to blush. "She's probably out for revenge on my father for saying no to her."

That didn't seem like the whole answer. Esi was definitely hiding something, but Darren didn't think it was the right moment to push. After all, he wasn't being fully truthful with her, either.

They were both quiet for a moment. Then Esi was the one to ask a question.

"Why do you think Sakura's after you—an *impundulu* with a cursed bloodline?"

Darren thought about his answer for a moment. He wanted to tell her the truth, that he *was* the *impundulu* connected to the First Four. He felt he could trust her, somehow.

But then he remembered Professor Zwane's warning—that Esi's father was one of the First Four's most outspoken critics. If only Darren knew *why*, he might be able to mend fences.

He was still weighing his response when the subway train took a curve and the overhead lights flickered. Darren jumped.

"That's normal," Esi said. "It happens all the time on these older trains. Don't wor—"

Esi's words were cut off by the *impundulu* from the

restaurant. Unfortunately, this one was not Professor Zwane. This was one of Sakura's followers. He smashed through the windowed door at the back of the car and shot a lightning bolt in their direction.

A murky haze filled the car as Esi let go with a stream of miasma. Whatever it was, it gently knocked out the few other people on the train.

Good, Darren thought. *The last thing we need is for a well-meaning nonmagical person to try to help us.*

"Follow me," Esi said, rushing to the other end of the car. She opened the door so that they could jump into the next subway car.

Darren ran backward, creating an electric force field to hold their attacker back. It worked for a few minutes, but the other *impundulu* had many more years of experience than Darren did. The field quickly started to weaken against the attacks coming their way. Darren wasn't going to be able to hold it in place much longer.

Esi turned, let the door go, and transformed. Even Darren was frightened by her transformation. Esi's Changer form was a massive tarantula with long, hairy legs. She kicked at the *impundulu*, seeming impervious to his lightning bolts. She played with him for a few minutes until he was totally exhausted. Then she immobilized her prey in a sticky web before filling the car with her miasma again, knocking him out.

Sakura's *impundulu* transformed back into his human form. He was curled up in the fetal position on a subway bench, looking to all the world as if he was fast asleep under a thick white blanket.

The massive spider turned and made her way back toward Darren, transforming when she reached his side.

The train slowed, and there was a garbled message over the PA system.

"What did they say?" Darren asked.

"Nothing important. We're coming to our stop," Esi answered.

The train slowed even more as it pulled into a station. People waited on the platform, and the nonmagical people in the car gathered their things and stepped toward the doors as if nothing had happened. No one even looked at the sleeping *impundulu* Changer as they walked past him. To them, he was simply another passenger.

The subway's doors opened.

Still overwhelmed by Esi's transformation, Darren stood frozen for a moment. She grabbed his hand and pulled him onto the platform.

Sakura's soldier stayed where he was, letting out a loud snore as the subway doors closed behind them.

Darren thought he heard Esi giggle as she yanked on his hand and jogged through the turnstile and up the stairs onto the street. Then she ducked into a side alley.

They stood behind a Dumpster, trying to catch their breath. Darren quickly threw up a force field around them.

Suddenly, Esi chuckled, and then laughed, until suddenly, she was cracking up.

Is *she hysterical?* Darren wondered. But it didn't seem like that kind of laughter. It sounded like Esi was having fun.

"Why on Earth are you laughing?" he asked.

Esi couldn't answer. She was laughing too hard. Tears streamed down her face, and she held her stomach.

Should I throw water at her or something? Darren thought. *Isn't that what you're supposed to do with hysterical people?*

Finally, Esi's laughter slowed enough that she was able to speak—between giggles. "My father never lets me out of his sight," she said. "Being in battle . . . It was such a rush! I've never gotten to try my moves outside of training. And on a real enemy! It was kind of . . . fun."

Darren chuckled despite himself. He had seen way too much of battle in the last year to share her sense of fun, but he could understand why Esi felt the way she did.

"You've got a weird definition of fun, Spider Girl," he said with a smile.

Esi let out one last giggle and then pointed uptown. "My cousin's apartment is just a few blocks that way," she said. "We'd better get moving before Sleeping Beauty wakes up and comes after us."

Darren smiled. Esi was starting to grow on him. She was much less intimidating than she'd seemed at first. "Lead the way," he said.

Chapter 8
A New Power

Gabriella sat slumped on a twin bed, blindly staring out of a hotel room window. On the bed closest to the door, Professor Zwane was looking at Margaery's arm. It had been badly burned in a burst of *kitsune* fire during their escape from the restaurant. And they had no idea where Darren was.

The professor thought Darren and Esi had gotten away in time, but Gabriella was worried. Esi's father was nowhere to be found either. Professor Zwane tried to contact him but turned up nothing. He thought the *anansi* leader had probably gone into hiding until things quieted down.

But what if he hasn't gone into hiding? What if he's captured or hurt? Instead of helping Darren, he'll blame him for the attack, she thought.

Gabriella felt like everything, Margaery's burns included, was all her fault.

I've failed two friends now, she thought. First I couldn't protect Mack from Sakura even after all of the special training my aunt and my grandmother gave me. And today I couldn't defend Darren. And now we don't even know where he is. Is he safe? Is he with Sakura?

Fiona sat down beside her friend with a take-out menu from a Chinese restaurant in her hand. "It's going to be okay," she told Gabriella with a reassuring smile. "The First Four said backup will be here soon. Once they get here, and Margaery's wing is healed, we can track down Darren."

Gabriella nodded, but she couldn't bring herself to answer or to smile in return. She couldn't even meet Fiona's eyes. That's if Darren is reachable, she thought.

"We'll be useless to Darren if we pass out from hunger. Will you tell me what you want for lunch?" Fiona asked. "You need to eat something."

"I can't eat," Gabriella said, the words catching in her throat. "Not when we haven't heard from Darren. It's been almost an hour. Why hasn't he texted?"

Because he's been snatched by Sakura's soldiers, she thought, answering her own question. She was afraid to voice her fears out loud.

Fiona could tell what her friend was thinking. "You know the First Four's rules," she said gently. "When you're separated from the group, get somewhere safe first and then check in. That's exactly what he's doing right now—finding safety and setting up protection. We'll hear from him soon."

"How can you be so sure?" Gabriella asked.

"Because Darren's defensive magic is the best there is. Plus, if he's with that *anansi* girl, there's no way the two of them could be taken down easily. Those spiders in the restaurant were *fierce*."

"What if her father found out about Darren's connection to the First Four? He could have handed him over to the enemy," Gabriella said.

Fiona shook her head vehemently. "Darren and Esi are probably—" Her phone buzzed. "It's Darren!"

Fiona quickly answered her cell. "Darren, you're on speaker," Fiona told him. "Please tell us you're all right. Gabriella, the professor, and Margaery are all here with me."

"I'm fine," Darren said. "I'm with Esi." He briefly described their escape from the restaurant and the battle on the subway. "We're at Esi's cousin's apartment. She isn't a Changer, but she knows about magic and everything."

"Are you safe there?" Gabriella asked.

"There are *anansi* protection spells on the apartment, so we'll be fine here until someone can pick us up. I don't think we should leave without reinforcements. Sakura's people might have tracked us here." Then he gave them the address.

"We're so relieved you're all right," Gabriella said.

"Me too. How's everything with you?" he asked. "Where are you?"

"We're stranded somewhere in Indiana," Fiona told him. "Waiting for backup to arrive."

"Why Indiana?" Darren asked.

"Mack burned Margaery's arm pretty badly during our escape," Fiona explained. "We were on our way back

pain when she was injured. Instead, she was in agony while we waited for help. Just one more thing I failed at today.

The *nahual* healer gently took Margaery's arm and then turned to Gabriella. "It's a pleasure to meet one of the Willow Cove younglings," he said to her. "We all owe you our freedom."

Gabriella didn't want his thanks or his praise; she just wanted him to heal her friend. And she wanted to learn from him if she could.

"Would you mind if I watch the healing?" she asked.

Margaery smiled through her pain. "Fine by me," she said.

"How does it work?" Gabriella asked Daniel.

"Have you used spiritual energy yet?" Daniel asked her as he examined the wound.

"I've spirit-walked, and I learned how to use defensive techniques while I'm spirit-walking, but I haven't trained in healing yet."

"It's unusual to find someone as young as you who has trained in the spiritual arts at all," Daniel said. "Healing is about channeling that same spiritual energy, but in the external world instead of inside the mind.

You have to make your energy solid but flexible."

"Solid but flexible?" Gabriella asked, confused.

"Once you experience it, it will make sense," Daniel said with a patient smile. "If you're too forceful, if you try too hard, it won't work. You have to allow your spirit energy to envelop the wound and find its own pathways into healing."

Daniel was silent for a moment. He closed his eyes and concentrated. Gabriella could see by his deep, even breathing that he had entered a meditative state.

"Once you've done that," he continued, passing his hand over Margaery's wound, "it's easy as pie. The body wants to heal itself. We're just helping it along."

Gabriella couldn't believe it. One second before, Margaery's arm had been blistered and burned, her skin blackened. Now she had a smooth, clean arm. There was absolutely no trace of the injury.

It's like it never happened, Gabriella thought. *What a beautiful power.*

Margaery breathed a big sigh of relief. The pain that was etched on her face disappeared. "Thank you, Daniel," she said.

The three of them joined the rest of the group. Professor Zwane and Fiona were just finishing up telling Miles Campagna, a bull who had helped them out before, about the battle in the restaurant.

Since they were still waiting for Yara and Ms. Therian to arrive with another *tengu* who could transport them while Margaery got her strength back, Gabriella and Daniel volunteered to pick up lunch from the Chinese restaurant two blocks away.

On their walk Gabriella asked the older *nahual* more questions about healing.

"The way you cured Margaery was really cool," Gabriella said. "I wish I could have known how to help her; at least how to lessen her pain while we waited."

"Healing is becoming a rarer and rarer skill," Daniel said. "But it's one that I've never regretted learning. I'll never stop being amazed and grateful for the gifts that I've been given."

Gabriella nodded. "I would like to master healing someday too," she said. "My grandmother and my aunt taught me to spirit-walk, but I know there's still so much more for me to learn."

"Healing magic doesn't seem to be all that interesting to young *nahuals* anymore. Everyone is focused on learning how to fight. They don't see that healing magic can be even more important than warrior skills. If only we could find a way to heal our differences instead of trying to battle our way to victory."

"Heal our differences?" Gabriella asked.

"I'm sure by now you've learned that not all fights are won by the strongest opponent. Sometimes it's the person who is smarter, or more determined, or has the most to lose. And sometimes the real winner is the one who is willing to concede."

Gabriella thought about what Daniel had said while they waited for their order. As soon as they had the food in hand and were on their way back, she picked up the conversation again.

"But in our war with Sakura, we can't concede," she said. "She's evil."

"That's true," Daniel said. "If fighting is truly the only way we can protect the ones we love, then it can't be avoided. But many of the old fights in the Changer world—between the *selkies* and the mermaids, or between the *anansis* and the *impundulus*—can be won if we embrace our differences and heal the old hurts that get in our way."

"I think I see what you mean," Gabriella said thoughtfully. "If we could all listen and understand one another, we wouldn't feel the need to fight. I hope when this war with Sakura is finished, we can get to work on that. I'd like to help make that happen. I know my friends would too."

"I believe you will, Gabriella," Daniel told her. "You kids are different from us. You might just change our world."

They had only just stepped inside the motel room when Yara and Ms. Therian arrived with the *tengu*, a young man, and a *mo'o*, a Hawaiian water dragon.

Gabriella had never seen Ms. Therian look so solemn, not even when Mack followed Sakura through her dark portal.

"Lunch will have to wait," Ms. Therian said. "Akira and Sefu will meet us in New York. We need to come up with a plan, a foolproof plan." She eyed the group gravely. "We've got to get to Darren before Sakura does, or we might never be able to save him."

Chapter 9
CIRCE'S DIADEM

Darren hung up the phone and turned to Esi and her cousin, Tani. "It won't be long," he said. "My friends will be here in a couple of hours with backup—as soon as Margaery, our *tengu* friend, is healed."

"Healed?" Tani asked. "What happened to her?"

"She was badly burned in the battle," Darren said. "But she's going to be fine."

Esi had been careful not to share too many details of the battle with her cousin. She only said that there had been trouble at the restaurant.

Nonmagical people tended to freak out when confronted with the harsher aspects of Changer life, and

Darren couldn't blame them. He still had trouble believing the fact that all these mythological creatures went to battle against one another on a regular basis. Now Tani held up her hand to stop them from telling her anything more. She clearly didn't want to hear it.

"I'll be in the kitchen," she said, backing out of the room. "You two talk about whatever you need to, but I don't . . . I don't want to know."

Esi smiled at her cousin, but she hadn't stopped pacing since they arrived in the apartment. She checked her phone. It was silent. She sent a text and waited for an answer that didn't come. Then she called, and Darren could tell by the look on her face that her father's phone had gone to voice mail—again.

She's really scared, Darren realized. *Maybe I can get her to think about something else while we're waiting to hear from her father.*

"So what's your school like?" Darren asked. "Are there other Changers in your classes?"

Esi wrinkled her nose. "It's a fancy New York City private school," she answered. "I wanted to try public school, but my dad said it was either private school or homeschooling."

"It must be so different growing up in a place like New York City," Darren said. "I live in a small town. There's one public middle school. If my parents wanted to send me to private school, I'd have to leave town."

"That must be kind of nice," Esi said.

Darren looked at her with a quizzical expression. "Having to leave town?"

"No, not leaving town—living someplace small. You must know a lot of people. Like, do you know your neighbors?"

"Of course. I see them all the time. How could you not know your neighbors?" Darren asked.

"You'd be surprised," Esi said with a laugh. "There are only four apartments on our floor, and I swear I've never seen anyone go in or out of one of them. I know someone lives there. Sometimes I can smell cooking in the hall, but I've never seen an actual person."

Darren laughed. "Maybe it's a hungry ghost."

"Speaking of hungry," Esi said. "Tani's kitchen is almost always stocked with the important food groups— root beer, ice cream, and whipped cream. Want a root beer float?"

"Sure," Darren said. "We were rudely interrupted at lunch after all."

He saw a cloud cross Esi's face as she remembered the fight and her father's disappearance.

He followed her into the kitchen, asking about her Changer training to keep her from worrying about her father again.

Tani was leaving the kitchen as they walked in. Esi's cousin seemed determined not to hear too much about that day's Changer activities.

"Do you get to hang out with other Changers in your training?" Darren asked.

"There are three other *anansi* younglings in the city," Esi said. "We train in an old soccer stadium on an island in the East River. Everyone else thinks it's abandoned."

"You don't train with other kinds of Changers?" Darren asked. "I work out with a *kitsune* and a *nahual*." He stopped himself before he could say "and a *selkie*," suddenly remembering that Esi didn't—and couldn't— know that he was from Willow Cove and connected to the First Four. "We learn a lot from one another."

Esi handed Darren a couple of tall glasses and a

carton of ice cream. He scooped vanilla into each glass, and then she added root beer and whipped cream.

"I wish I knew more Changers," Esi said. "My dad's been pretty mistrustful of anyone who isn't *anansi*. And it's only gotten worse since Sakura reemerged."

"He seemed willing to help me, though," Darren offered.

Esi's voice tightened. "The *impundulus* are a strategic ally for us. He has a good reason to want to break the curses."

"Were you at the Youngling Games at Wyndemere in the spring?" Darren asked.

"No," Esi said, taking a spoonful of her root beer float. "We were visiting relatives in Ghana. I really want to go to Wyndemere for high school, though. I've heard all about it from my aunt."

Darren stirred the ice cream around in his glass. Esi's life sounded really lonely. She didn't have many other Changers to talk to, and she hadn't mentioned any non-magical friends. "Maybe your dad will let you train with me sometime," Daren said hopefully. "When this is all over."

"Maybe," Esi said, draining her glass. She checked her phone for texts, but there were none. So she dialed her father again. "Why isn't he answering?" she asked. "Why hasn't he gotten in touch with me?"

"Don't worry," Darren told her with a confidence he didn't really feel. "I'm sure he made it out okay."

"I'm not worried about *him*," Esi said. "I just don't want him to worry about *me*."

Everything about her behavior proved that she *was* worried about her father, but Darren didn't challenge her statement. He simply waited for her to say more.

"My father is the strongest, most powerful *anansi* I know. There's no way he'd go down or even get hurt in a battle against such small fries as those Changers in the restaurant."

"Okay," Darren said with a wry smile. "So why haven't you stopped pacing and checking your phone since we arrived?"

"I'm not sure what he'd want me to do right now. The *anansi* alliance pretty much fell apart when some of the families decided to go over to Sakura. My father told me not to trust *anyone* outside the family."

"You're with your cousin," Darren said. "So you're doing exactly what he told you to do."

"I'm also with you—an *impundulu* that was cursed by one of our ancestors. I'm not sure he'd like that. And Tani's not a Changer. She can't help me if Sakura's soldiers come back. And I don't want to put her in danger."

"You're welcome to come back to Willow Cove with me," Darren said quickly. "You'll be safe there until we find your father."

Esi stopped pacing and faced him. Her expression completely changed. "Willow Cove? So my father was right," she said. "You *are* part of that group of younglings working with the First Four."

Uh-oh, Darren thought. I *wasn't supposed to tell her that. . . . But I guess the cat's out of the bag now.*

"I am," Darren said quietly.

Esi eyed him in mock surprise. "I knew it," she said. Then she sized him up. "There are rumors that you and your friends are going to be the next First Four," she said, cocking an eyebrow.

Darren shook his head, but he didn't feel comfortable lying to her outright.

Now Esi took on a teasing tone. "But judging from how useless you were in our subway fight, there's no way that could be true."

"Hey," Darren said, laughing. "I kept that *impundulu* at bay until you could knock him out with your magical miasma."

Wow, as worried as she is, she's still able to joke around. She's strong. I've never met anyone as cool and confident as her before.

Then he got more serious. "So it's an easy guess why Sakura is after *me*. Now it's your turn to come clean. Why is Sakura *really* after you?"

They were interrupted by a knock on the apartment door. Esi ran over and peeked through the peephole. "It's my father!" she said.

Before Darren could stop her, she threw open the door and jumped into her father's outstretched arms, breaking the *anansi* protection spells they had activated around the apartment.

"I'm so glad you're all right," she said. "I've been worried."

Esi's father awkwardly patted her on the back. The

guards around him were completely silent. No one smiled. No one seemed relieved. No one said a word.

Something's not right, Darren thought. He got a sick feeling in his stomach.

One of the guards pulled Esi away from her father, locking his arms around her shoulders and clamping a hand over her mouth.

The illusion they were using dissolved.

Instead of Esi's father's bodyguard, one of Sakura's *nykurs* had the girl in his grasp. And Esi's father was really Mack, now openly smirking at Darren. He was surrounded not by *anansi* bodyguards but by more of Sakura's soldiers.

"Remember me?" Mack asked with a sneer.

"Mack," Darren answered, trying to stay cool even as he stumbled backward. Of course it was Mack, but the mean expression he wore didn't look like Mack at all. "It's time for you to come home, Mack. You're grandfather misses you—we all do."

Mack threw his head back and laughed. "You have no idea of the power I'd be giving up if I did that. It's not gonna happen. But you—you could join us. Darren, we can help you become the most powerful *impundulu* of all time."

Darren shook his head and echoed Mack's words. "Not gonna happen," he said.

While Mack and Darren were talking, Esi struggled to get away from her captor. She bit his hand, and he yanked it away with a yelp. That was all the opening she needed. She jerked her head back and forth, blowing her paralyzing miasma at the group. The *nykur* holding her fell to the floor, unconscious. But Mack managed to jump out of her way just in time.

In the confusion, Darren concentrated on bringing electricity to the tips of his fingers. The sparks came together, and he threw up a force field, pushing Mack farther into the hallway with the others. Even after everything Mack had done, Darren couldn't bring himself to hurt his friend. Esi scrambled back into the apartment while the others were distracted.

Before Mack's fire arrows could pierce his protections, Darren slammed the door and extended the force field to the whole apartment.

"There's no way this is just revenge against the

anansis because your father didn't join her army," Darren said to Esi. "Be honest with me. Something else is going on here. I told you why they're looking for me. What does Sakura want with you?"

Esi was about to answer when Tani came into the room, pale and trembling. "What's going on?" she asked.

"Can you take the fire escape down and wait for me at our special place in the park?" Esi asked. "I can't explain right now, but I'm not sure you'll be safe here. At least not until we find my father."

"I'm not going without you," Tani said. "Your father would never forgive me."

"My father will understand," Esi said. "I have to stay here."

"You just said it's not safe," her cousin answered.

"I'm fine for now, but we can't protect you. You'll be safe in the park. They're not after you."

Tani hesitated. There was a kick at the door, and she jumped.

"Go now," Esi urged.

"Help is on the way," Darren assured her. "Esi will be fine, but you shouldn't be here."

"Okay," Tani said. "Call or come to me as soon as you can."

"I will," Esi promised with a shaky smile.

Tani tried to smile back, but she wasn't quite successful.

Darren lowered the force field at the window in front of the fire escape and opened it for her.

"Be safe," Tani said, and climbed out the window.

Darren raised the force field again. He and Esi watched Tani make her way down the ladder to the street.

Interruptions had kept Esi from answering Darren's question twice now. He wouldn't be put off again. He repeated his question. "What does Sakura want with you?"

Esi sighed. She opened her mouth to answer, then hesitated.

"We're about to go into battle again," Darren said. "I'd like to know what I'm fighting for. I deserve to know."

"They want this." Esi reluctantly pulled a stone-hewn circlet out of her satchel. It looked like a crown of some kind, although a simple one. Still, it was beautiful in its simplicity.

Darren reached out to touch it, but before he could take it in his hand, someone started to pound on the apartment door—hard.

"What is it?" Darren asked, trying to ignore the noise.

"This is one of the Changers' most powerful relics—Circe's Diadem. The wearer can awaken magical potential sleeping inside nonmagical people."

Darren had learned about Circe. She was the magical being who first awakened transformative magic in ordinary humans who needed her help.

Darren touched the rough stone. It was surprisingly warm, like there was life in it.

"So Circe's Diadem can create new Changers?" Darren asked.

Esi nodded sheepishly. "Or magic-users. But only in people who already have the potential. Sometimes because of curses or other reasons, people don't develop their gifts naturally. This makes sure that they do."

"But why do you have it? Why isn't it locked away in a vault somewhere?" Darren asked. "Especially with Sakura on the loose. Think of the damage she could cause, turning new Changers over to the dark side before they even know what's happening to them." He felt himself getting angry at the thought. "That's just flat-out dangerous."

It was Esi's turn to be embarrassed. "You're not the first *impundulu* who came to me seeking forgiveness. I guess my ancestors were pretty generous with their curses. I tried to give the *impundulus* what they wanted: to accept their apologies and forgive them so that the curses would be broken."

"So why didn't you?" Darren asked.

"I tried, but for the magic to work, I have to really mean it. I have to really feel forgiveness," she explained. "But how can I forgive someone I hardly know for something one of their ancestors did hundreds of years ago? It wasn't working."

Darren's shoulders slumped. The pounding on the door had stopped for a few moments, but now it started up again. Louder than before. He had to concentrate to hold the force field in place. He also had to shout to be heard. "So when you try to break the curses, it doesn't work?"

"No," Esi admitted, shouting back. "The *impundulus*

who came to us were getting angry and disappointed. But my father knew about this relic. He used magic to find it somehow; I don't know how or where. So I've been using the diadem to awaken the powers of the cursed *impundulus'* relatives one by one. It's really just a Band-Aid for the problem, but it satisfied the last few Changers who asked for help."

The real essence of what Esi had just said hit Darren so hard that he was breathless for a second. "So you can't lift my curse even if you want to?" he asked.

"No," Esi admitted. "I can try, but I don't think it will work. It hasn't before."

Darren tried not to let panic overtake him.

If I can't escape the curse, my ancestors won't be able to protect me from Sakura. I'll be on my own with no way to fight against her mind control. She'll turn me into one of her evil soldiers, fighting alongside Mack. This is bad. . . . This is very, very bad.

In that moment Darren's fear created a chink in his force field.

That was all Mack and the others needed. With one last deafening push, they crashed through the door.

Chapter 10
THE WOUND

Gabriella rattled off the address of Esi's cousin's apartment to the *tengu*, Kenta, and they arrived with Yara, Ms. Therian, Fiona, the *nahual* healer Daniel, and the *mo'o*.

"Apartment buildings are tricky," Ms. Therian said. "It's hard to suddenly appear unnoticed."

"Can't you use magic to erase the nonmagical peoples' memories?" Gabriella asked. "Yara does that all the time."

"We don't want to cause a panic," Yara said. "Even if it's a panic we can undo. It would alert the enemy to our position and allow them the time they need to call for reinforcements."

"We can't give them that time," Ms. Therian added. "Remember, we could land right in the middle of a battle, already outnumbered."

"I may have a solution." Kenta closed his eyes and concentrated for a moment. Then he disappeared. "The elevator is empty," he said when he reappeared suddenly. "It just left the lobby for the fourteenth floor. We can land there."

"Which floor is Darren on?" Margaery asked.

"He's on the third floor. Apartment 3F," Gabriella answered.

"Let's go now, before the elevator gets to fourteen and someone gets on," Kenta said.

Margaery was still worried about her ability to carry everyone so soon after her arm was injured, so they all put a hand on Kenta's shoulder instead. Gabriella felt the familiar *whoosh*, followed by silence. They were cushioned in the calm center of an invisible wind. Mostly calm, anyway. Gabriella noticed that Kenta's ride wasn't quite as smooth as Margaery's.

They arrived in the elevator in a matter of seconds. It dipped and then continued upward. It was just passing the tenth floor.

Yara recited a spell under her breath and pushed the button for three. The elevator reversed course.

A burst of noise greeted them when the elevator's doors opened. Two of Sakura's people, a *nykur* and an *impundulu*, were unconscious on the floor in the hall surrounded by splinters of wood. The apartment door had been ripped from its hinges.

A major battle was going on inside apartment 3F.

Ms. Therian nodded to the *mo'o*, who produced two pairs of magical shackles to further immobilize the unconscious fighters. Then Gabriella's coach and teacher transformed before entering the apartment. If a giant werewolf jumping into the fray surprised any of the fighters, they didn't show it.

The rest of the group followed Ms. Therian into the apartment. Gabriella and Fiona brought up the rear.

Gabriella was about to step into the apartment when Yara put up a hand to stop her. "Mack is here," she whispered. "Can you spirit-walk and try to reach him again? You came close to turning him around in the restaurant."

"I'll try," Gabriella agreed. "He might be watching for me more closely now, though."

"That will be difficult for him in the midst of battle," Yara told her. "He'll be too distracted to guard his mind. You should be able to slip in while he's focused on protecting himself from physical assaults."

"I'll do my best."

"Of course you will." Yara smiled at her, drew a wall of water around herself, and stepped into the apartment.

Gabriella stayed in the hall. She peeked inside to see a massive battle underway. She felt like she needed to get a visual on Mack before she meditated.

Darren and a girl were in the middle of the chaos, fighting back-to-back against Mack and the others. Darren was mostly focused on Mack. He tried to surround him with an electrical field, but Mack broke it apart with a dark flame.

Gabriella recognized Esi from the spell in Professor Zwane's office. While she watched, the girl blew of cloud of something at a *nykur*, and it collapsed to the floor, instantly changing into its human form. Before Gabriella could even react, the *mo'o* was at his side to clap him in magical chains.

Darren and Esi had definitely been outnumbered.

Help arrived just in time, Gabriella thought.

Ms. Therian and the others had turned the tide of the battle, but Mack and the rest of Sakura's forces were still putting up a good fight.

There was no time to lose. Gabriella had to block out all the noise, all the chaos, and all her worries or she'd fail. She found a corner in the hallway and slipped into the meditative state that would allow her to spirit-walk into Mack's mind.

Maybe this time I can remind him who he really is—the fun-loving kid whose comic book superheroes always defeat evil in the end. The goodness that's still inside him can defeat Sakura's wickedness—it has to.

Moments later, in her spirit form, Gabriella left her body behind and entered into the apartment. Mack was at the center of the fight. He seemed to be relishing every second of the chaos and destruction he was causing. There was a kind of demented pleasure radiating from him when one of his arrows hit its target.

Next Gabriella entered into Mack's mind. Her spirit self always took her *nahual* form at first, but now she transformed into her human self. It was easier to go unnoticed that way. She stayed at the edges of Mack's thoughts and memories, hoping to get a hold on him before he spotted her and tried to push her out. Then she did again what had almost worked in the restaurant: she found Mack's happiest memories, the ones that hadn't yet been infected by Sakura, and tried to bring them to the forefront of his mind.

It wasn't long before Mack's shadow self found her. She had to battle with him using her spiritual energy or be pushed out of his mind. At that moment Fiona surrounded Mack with water, trying to keep him safe from an attack by Kenta.

In his need to dodge Kenta's attack and get away from Fiona, Mack momentarily forgot all about Gabriella.

Like Fiona, Gabriella didn't want to hurt Mack, only subdue him. He and his shadow self were intricately connected.

This is Mack, she reminded herself. *Our Mack. If I destroy his shadow self, will I destroy the goodness in him too? This is tricky.*

She was overwhelmed by the pain and anger that Sakura had filled Mack with when she turned him evil.

Despair emanated from almost every part of him. It colored even his happiest memories. Gabriella could feel it like an open wound. And that's when it hit her.

He's in terrible pain—just like Margaery was. Only this pain is in his mind, not his body. Mack's inner shadow fox isn't something to fight; it's something to heal!

Mack tried to push Gabriella out of his mind again, but she stood her ground. Then his attention was turned away . . . to the physical battle he was fighting. This was her chance.

It's now or never, Gabriella told herself. *You might not get an opportunity like this again.*

Gabriella had never tried to use her spiritual energy to heal before, but she had to at least try. She channeled her energy like Daniel had showed her. She saw it as warm and glowing, flexible enough to find its own way to put the broken pieces of Mack back together.

She saw the light-filled, peaceful energy move through Mack's mind, searching for places to heal.

Daniel said that the body wants to heal itself, she remembered. *The mind must want that too.*

The energy moved through Mack, healing memory

by memory. The despair and hopelessness were leaving him. She could feel it. The light absorbed the darkness and rendered it helpless.

Mack figured out what was happening. He turned on her and howled in rage with the last bits of darkness inside him, but he couldn't stop the flow of the healing energy. His rage dissipated almost as soon as he felt it.

It's working! It's working! Gabriella realized.

She concentrated on sending that warm, glowing spirit to every corner of Mack's mind. It moved in and out of his memories, turning darkness to light.

And then she saw it!

The shadowy flames gave way to bright oranges and yellows. *Mack is coming back to us. He's returning to his old self!*

Chapter 11
THE SPY

Mack was in midattack. He had evaporated the *selkie's* wall of water with a sneer.

"I don't need your protection!" he shouted at her. "But you're going to wish you had protection from me."

He turned his back on her, to show her just how little he feared her, and burned a hole in the *anansi* girl's miasma. He was about to completely disable her; thoughts of the praise he would receive when he dropped her at Sakura's feet filled his mind.

Well done, apprentice, she'd say. And then she'd tell the rest of her followers to bow to his greatness.

But he was snatched out of his daydream by a sudden,

sharp pain in his head. He felt like there was something inside him, trying to rip him in two.

It's that nahual, he realized. *She's walking around in my mind again.*

He felt his glorious power softening, and howled in rage. He cast around for her so that he could throw her out. He had done it once; he'd do it again.

I'm more powerful than she'll ever be, he told himself. *I'm strong enough to stand alone at Sakura's side. The nahual needs the others and the First Four to prop her up. She's weak, just like they are.*

But he felt a sudden rush of happiness run through him, and he no longer wanted to see her gone. Memories of hanging out with his friends flooded him—creating comic books with Joel so that they could show them at the art fair, battling Auden Ironbound on the beach and winning, discovering that he had earned a second tail. And then, hanging out with his Changer friends—including the *nahual*—in their secret gym at school.

He saw the two of them in the comic book they created together—battling evil and winning. Joyfully celebrating their victories.

He thought he had left joy behind when he joined Sakura. But now he felt it again—a spark of happiness. Happiness and more. He felt hope, too. It wasn't the dark anticipation that he would rule by Sakura's side and wreak chaos in the world. It was a light-filled hope that he would once again be with his friends and family.

Then his grandfather was there, standing in front of him in his *kitsune* form. His expression was one of love and compassion.

Jiichan! Mack thought. Love swelled in his heart. He had missed his grandfather more than he'd known.

Jiichan's fur was as white as fresh snow. Mack knew if he reached out to touch it, it would be as soft as a cloud. The white *kitsune* stood, ready to embrace Mack.

But then Sakura bounded in front of Mack and faced off against his grandfather. Her sleek black coat stood in sharp contrast to his white one. She oozed darkness and despair, but the overwhelming feeling Mack got from her was rage.

Mack was suddenly frightened—not for himself, but for his grandfather.

His new master with her jet-black fur and seven

tails wrestled for the upper hand, but Jiichan was just as strong, if not stronger. He was older, of course, but more experienced in battle. And he had acquired nine tails—the maximum—in his long life. Sakura still had only seven.

The two *kitsunes* circled each other wordlessly. Jiichan's face was full of calm determination. Sakura's, full of wrath and reckless fury.

Mack drifted in and out of consciousness, unable to tell what was really happening and what he was imagining. Was the *nahual* planting false memories in his mind?

Warmth battled with despair inside him; love with rage. He felt himself beginning to collapse and transform back into his human body. This was a Change he wasn't able to resist.

Has the anansi *girl's poison gotten to me?* he wondered.

Just before he transformed he thought he heard Sakura scream at his grandfather.

"What made *him* so special?" she yelled. "Why did *he* get that power? The power that should have been mine? Who decided?"

Mack started to drift off into something like sleep. In the great white space of his mind, he found Gabriella. He reached out to her, and they hugged.

"It's me," Mack told her. "I'm back. I'm—"

The profound calm he'd felt just a second ago dissipated, and he remembered all the horrible things he'd done in the last few weeks. He remembered with a rush of guilt that he'd hurt Margaery just that day.

"I'm so sorry for everything," he said, burying his head in his hands. "The things I said, the things I did . . ."

"You weren't yourself," Gabriella said with a smile. "We all know that. And that's past now. We don't ever have to think about it again."

"I still can't believe you did it," Mack said. "How did you undo Sakura's spell?"

Gabriella looked serious for a moment. "Sakura's magic inflicts pain to whatever it touches. I learned a bit about how healing and spirit-walking magic are two sides of the same coin, so I just . . . put them together."

"Pain . . . ," Mack said, realizing something.

"Mack, I'm so happy for you," Gabriella broke into his thoughts. "We've missed you."

Mack transformed into his *kitsune* form. His third, shadowy tail was gone. His fur was snow white again. He was truly himself once more. He could rejoin the fight of good versus evil—on the right side.

He transformed back into his human self so he could talk to Gabriella more easily.

And in that transformation, Mack made a big decision.

"You know what I have to do," he said to her.

"You have to come home with us," she insisted.

"No," Mack said. "I have to do my best to make sure Sakura loses this war. I can't do that if I come back with you."

Gabriella shook her head. She knew the real Mack— the brave, stubborn, too-ambitious Mack—well enough to know what he was thinking. Tears ran down her cheeks. "You don't have to do anything, Mack. Come back with me."

I want that more than anything, Mack thought. *But this is too important.*

Mack smiled at his friend. "The only way to take Sakura down is to do it from the inside," he said. "She's too tricky, too smart, and way too determined. You'll need inside information to win."

"It's dangerous," Gabriella told him. "We could lose you again. You could lose yourself."

"I have to do this," he answered simply. "You know it, and I know it."

This is how I can thank Gabriella for saving me, Mack thought. *This is how I can make it up to the others—all the wrong I did under Sakura's control. And how I can thank Jiichan for being the best, most loving grandfather I could have had.*

"You're no longer a shadow fox," Gabriella said. "Sakura will see your white fur. She'll notice the missing tail. Whatever else she is, she's *smart*."

"She is smart, but so am I," Mack said. "She taught me something really important—illusion. It took a while, but I'm a good student. I mastered it."

He closed his eyes for a moment, concentrating. When he transformed this time, he changed back into his shadow self, complete with a third tail. *Don't worry,* he communicated telepathically. *I'm still me.*

He transformed back and smiled at her.

"I can hide who I really am—at least until the time is right. She's had such a strong hold on me that I don't think she'll suspect anything's wrong. She's too consumed with seeking revenge on my grandfather. She's blinded to almost everything else but that."

"But what can you do with her that you can't do fighting by our sides?" Gabriella asked. "Why do you have to stay with her?"

"So I can send you information about the Shadow Fox's army and its movements. We'll take her down much more quickly this way. I know we will."

Gabriella's eyes welled with tears again. "But I *saved* you," she said, falling to her knees. "I healed you. I finally did it. You can't leave."

"I'm so grateful," Mack said. "You *did* save me. You don't know how much I want to go home, but I have to do this. This is the best way I know to make up for all the pain I caused."

"You didn't," Gabriella said. "Sakura did. Don't blame yourself."

"But this was my fault," Mack said. "I was impatient. My grandfather told me to stay away from her—you all did—and I went after her by myself at Wyndemere. I thought I could deal with her one-on-one. That was a huge mistake, and that's how she got to me."

"Don't you want to see your grandfather first?" she said.

Mack shook his head. He knew that would be too hard. *I don't know if I'm strong enough to leave him again,* Mack thought. *It's better if I don't see him.*

"Tell Jiichan I'll see him soon," Mack said. "Tell him I learned from my mistakes. Tell him I called him Jiji," he added, using the pet name he'd called his grandfather when he was really little.

Before Gabriella could object again, Mack called up a burst of power and ejected her from his mind.

Bye, Gabriella, he thought. *Thanks for saving me. I'll do everything I can to help you defeat the Shadow Fox.*

Chapter 12
Aftermath

Fiona encased Mack in a bubble of water the minute he fell into unconsciousness and transformed. She didn't want to see her friend hurt, but she also couldn't let him get away.

Daniel, the *nahual*, had proved to be an expert fighter. He was approaching Mack with a set of magical chains when Mack woke up. He transformed into his shadowy *kitsune* form and instantly turned Fiona's water bubble into mist with his dark flames.

Then he leaped between Sakura and his grandfather, his back to Mr. Kimura, stopping their uneasy dance. Fiona saw some kind of telepathic communication between Sakura and Mack, but they shielded it from everyone around them.

Mack didn't even look at his grandfather, Fiona thought. *But he doesn't seem nearly as angry as he did earlier. Something's different. Something's changed.*

Fiona looked around for Gabriella, but her friend was still in the hall. The battle seemed to be winding down, but they had to keep their guards up—especially now that Sakura had appeared. None of the First Four's followers had been captured, but a few of Sakura's soldiers were in chains.

While Fiona watched, Sakura waved her tails in a circle, and a dark portal opened up behind her, just like the one she had opened in Willow Cove when she first took Mack away. At the end of that fight, Sakura had pulled Mack in with her. This time, he was the first one to jump through.

He looked over his shoulder and flashed Fiona with a wicked smile.

Before she could respond, Sakura's other minions, those that hadn't been captured, rushed into the portal after Mack. Sakura stood alone, her eyes on Mr. Kimura.

He raised a paw, ready to attack. But in the blink of an eye, Sakura joined her soldiers and the portal closed behind her.

The battle was over. Mack was gone—again.

The remaining Changers began to examine their wounds. Daniel went from Changer to Changer, healing whatever needed to be healed.

Darren and Esi headed to the park to meet her cousin, and hopefully, her father.

Ms. Therian and Yara cast spells to put the apartment back to rights. Gabriella stepped into the room just as the door magically came together and covered the entrance to the apartment.

Miles and the *mo'o* helped the others wrestle their prisoners to Kenta for transport.

"Can you get the others back home?" Kenta asked Margaery.

She smiled and raised her previously injured arm, showing him her muscles. "Don't worry about me," she said. "I'm tough."

"We'll get these traitors to prison, then," he said. A second later he and the prisoners had disappeared.

With Sakura's soldiers gone, Fiona felt free to talk.

"Something felt different about Mack just before he left. It was like he was himself again. But that can't be true, can it?" she asked Mr. Kimura. "He fought for Sakura, and he left with her. The real Mack would never do that."

"Were you able to reach him at all?" she asked, turning to Gabriella.

Gabriella took a shaky breath.

She looks exhausted, Fiona thought. *What battles did she have to wage in Mack's mind?*

"I felt it too," Mr. Kimura said. "Gabriella, you succeeded in bringing our Makoto back, didn't you?"

"I did. It was actually thanks to Daniel," Gabriella said, nodding toward the far corner of the room, where Daniel was healing another injured fighter. "He taught me about healing, and that was when I realized that that's exactly what Mack needed. Dark magic isn't like Changer magic. It's full of pain. It feels like something that needs to be healed, not conquered. I decided to try that with Mack."

"And it worked," Mr. Kimura said. "You are wise beyond your years, Gabriella." He looked toward Fiona.

"All four of you have a wisdom and bravery that consistently impresses me for ones so young."

"But I'm confused," Fiona said. "Did Sakura succeed in turning Mack again? His fur was still dark like that ... And if he's healed, why did he go back with Sakura? Why didn't he stay so he can help us defeat her?"

"I tried to get him to stay," Gabriella said. "I pleaded with him, but he thinks he can do more good for us from the inside. He said he learned illusion from Sakura, so he's able to make himself look like a shadow fox, even though he isn't one. And he said that staying close to Sakura is the best way to defeat her."

"He's right," Yara said. "He can help us win this war from the inside, from the very center of Sakura's lair. He'll have access to vital information he can pass along to us. It's genius, really, that he thought of it."

"Won't that be dangerous?" Fiona asked. "It's not like he's a *real* superhero. He's a youngling Changer just like the rest of us. What if Sakura figures it out? What if he gets caught? She could ... "

Fiona didn't need to finish her sentence. Every one of them knew the dangers.

"He said he's mastered illusion magic," Gabriella said. "We have no choice but to trust him in this. I couldn't clap him in chains and force him to stay. He wants to help us, and this was the best way he could think of."

Fiona shuddered. *I hate the thought of him spending one more second with Sakura than he has to. What if he gets caught? Or worse, what if Sakura turns him again? If he's mastered illusion magic, how will we even know?*

"We'll need all the help we can get if we have any chance of succeeding against Sakura," Ms. Therian said. "Mack's inside information will make a big difference. Sakura's numbers are rising."

Mr. Kimura was quiet but seemed resigned to Mack's decision.

Ms. Therian moved away to help Yara put the rest of Tani's apartment back together, leaving Fiona and Gabriella alone with Mr. Kimura.

"Thank you for what you did for Makoto," he said to Gabriella.

"He wanted you to know how sorry he is," Gabriella said. "He talked about how much he had learned from his mistakes and how he was going to do better in the future. That's a big part of why he went back with Sakura—so he could make up for the hurt he caused."

Mr. Kimura was quiet and thoughtful, his head bowed.

Gabriella could feel his sadness, but she didn't think that was something she could heal. The only thing that would heal Mr. Kimura's pain was to have Mack at his side again.

"He wanted you to know how grateful he is," Gabriella added softly. She could feel herself on the verge of tears. "He said to be sure to tell you he called you Jiji and that he'd see you soon."

Mack's grandfather gave Gabriella a hug, his own eyes overflowing. "Thank you," he said. He reached for Fiona and pulled her into the circle. "Thanks to both of you for believing in Makoto."

"We'll get him back," Fiona said, wiping away a tear of her own. "We'll defeat Sakura, and we'll bring Mack home."

Chapter 13
Forgiveness

The minute Sakura disappeared through her dark portal, Esi wanted to go to the park to find her cousin and—she hoped—her father. Darren couldn't let her go alone. He let the others know where to find him and followed Esi down the fire escape just in case.

Darren was relieved to see that she still carried the bag with Circe's Diadem inside. He had forgotten about it in the heat of battle. Its magic would be disastrous in Sakura's hands.

When they reached the bottom, Esi opened her bag and showed him the ancient relic again. "I don't want the others to see, but you can borrow the diadem if you want," she said. "I trust you. I know you won't use it the wrong way."

Darren wasn't sure he did want it. *Even if Ray is a Changer, he can't lift the curse on us or protect me from Sakura. I'll be putting him in danger—at least until this war is over—by giving him the choice to have Changer powers.*

"It's probably not a good idea right now," Darren said.

"You're right," Esi said, putting it back into her bag. Then she took a deep breath. "I hope you do find a way to break the curse. For what it's worth, I forgive you for whatever your ancestors did to mine."

"Thanks," Darren said, though he realized how hollow the words felt.

"It's silly to hold a grudge for a thousand years. I know that, even if my ancestors didn't. But my forgiveness probably won't do you any good," Esi said. "No one else I forgave ever had their curse lifted."

Darren shrugged. "I know you would break the curse if you could. That means a lot. Professor Zwane is working hard to find another way. That, or to find another spell that will protect me from Sakura's mind control."

He eyed the diadem again. "You should keep that, but not in your purse. You and your father need to find a safe place for it and guard it with protection spells. If it falls into the wrong hands . . ." Darren's voice trailed off while he thought about the disastrous consequences the diadem could cause in the hands of Sakura or one of her followers.

"We'll find a safe place for it," Esi said. "Sakura won't get the diadem. I promise."

They walked toward the park. After the intense battle in Tani's apartment, the busy streets didn't seem nearly as hectic or as loud as they had earlier. None of the nonmagical people around them could possibly guess that the two of them had just been in a major battle. Esi, in her yellow sundress, still looked like a cool, carefree New York City girl.

It was hard to believe that barely an afternoon had passed since Darren landed in that parking lot. He was beginning to feel like he had known Esi for a very long time.

"So," Darren said awkwardly as they neared the park, "I know you said your dad doesn't let you out much, but maybe you could come to Willow Cove and train with us sometime." He could feel his face getting hot, and he hoped Esi wouldn't notice that he was blushing.

Esi laughed. "Now that my dad thinks that you're part of the new First Four? There's no way he'd allow that."

"Even though the First Four just risked their lives in battle to protect the two of us from Sakura?" he asked.

Esi shrugged, embarrassed.

"What's his problem with the First Four?" Darren asked. "Do you know?"

"I don't," Esi said. "It's another one of those grudges that goes way back."

"There are too many of those in the Changer world," Darren said. "We need to find a way to work together—for good. Our generation has to do a better job."

"Maybe you're right," Esi said.

"The new First Four are going to need allies, counselors. . . . We're still learning, but we do want to lead better. To do that, we have to get to know other Changers and find out what they want."

"*Anansis* are different from other Changers. You can't just lump us all together."

"I don't want to," Darren said. "I want to learn about the different *anansi* families, and your history. You can teach me."

Esi smiled. "You have a lot to learn," she teased.

"So do you," Darren teased back. "You're wrong about the other Changers. They aren't blind followers of the First Four. And I can teach you that whatever problem your father has with their leadership can be solved. I'll see to it."

"Give me your phone," Esi said with a challenge in her eyes.

Darren handed it over. Esi scrolled through his apps and then typed something.

"Here," she said, handing it back. "You just friended me on InstaInstaChat. We can be pen pals until we go to Wyndemere Academy together."

Darren was about to ask her if her dad was really going to let her go away to school—he seemed more than a little overprotective—when they stepped into the park. In seconds they saw what looked like Esi's dad and his guards standing with Esi's cousin, Tani.

Esi's father rushed toward his daughter.

"Are you all right?" he asked Esi. "When I found Tani here by herself I thought the worst."

"I've been worried about you, too," Esi said. "Where have you been? Why didn't you call or text?"

"Some of Sakura's soldiers followed us from the restaurant. Until we were sure we lost them, I thought it was too dangerous to be in touch. I didn't want them to use me to track you down."

"I'm fine, Dad," Esi told him. "Sakura and her minions showed up, but Darren and I fought them off together. And just when I thought we were going to lose and end up as Sakura's prisoners, the First Four showed up to help."

"The First Four? To help you?" Esi's father couldn't hide his surprise.

"They came to our rescue," Esi said. "I don't know what would have happened if they hadn't. And I couldn't have done any of it without Darren."

Esi's father turned to Darren and shook his hand. "Thank you," he said. "I'm sorry if I was rude earlier. I meant no offense. I'll do whatever you need to help you break the curse."

Should I tell him that his daughter already offered her for-giveness? Darren wondered. *Or will that get Esi into trouble?*

He hoped to get some sort of signal from Esi herself, but her face was blank.

"Thank you," Darren said finally. "Professor Zwane is looking into some other options for my protection. We don't want a lot of new people suddenly transforming into *impundulus* while we're in the middle of a war."

Mr. Akosua seemed impressed. "I think that's wise," he said. "If I can help Sidima in any way, I'll be happy to."

Wow, am I winning him over? Darren thought, shocked. *Maybe there's real hope for Changer peace when this war with Sakura is finished.*

Before Darren had a chance to say thank you, there was a ripple in the wind, and Fiona and Gabriella appeared with Margaery.

"Ready to go?" Fiona asked. "We have to get back."

Darren nodded and took hold of the *tengu's* arm.

"Later, Spider Girl," he said, giving Esi a quick wave before he disappeared.

EPILOGUE

Darren got home in time for dinner, just like he promised. After Fiona and Gabriella filled him in on what had happened with Mack, he trudged up the front walk feeling as if the longest day of his life was coming to an end. He was grateful for the First Four's protection spells. He was more tired than he had ever been, and he couldn't wait to get inside and let his guard down.

He opened the front door and flipped on the hall light.

Nothing happened.

He flipped it off and on, off and on. Still nothing.

Is *the power out?* he wondered. He peered out the

window and saw that Mrs. Wood's lights were on across the street, and so were the Davises' next door. *It's just my house*, he realized.

"Anyone home?" Darren yelled.

No one answered.

He took out his cell to call his mom and find out where she was, but he noticed a flickering light coming from the end of the hallway.

Something's wrong. Has Sakura found a way to get past the protection spells the First Four put on the house?

Darren brought electricity to the tips of his fingers and then drew them back in a big circle. When he was encased in a protective force field, he started down the hall. He turned the corner into the family room, expecting the worst.

Instead, he saw Ray standing in the middle of the room. An electric current was running up and down his arms. He looked more frightened than Darren had ever seen him look before.

Ray looked up and caught his brother's eye.

"Darren!" Ray shouted. "Stay back!"

What challenge will the Changers face next?

Here is a sneak peek at

THE HIDDEN WORLD OF
Changers

The Changer War

Fiona Murphy had just returned home from a long, exhausting day in New York City. Perhaps the average girl would have been excited to visit New York City, but Fiona was hardly the "average girl."

Fiona was a *selkie*, a magical shape-shifting Changer who could transform into a seal. Up until her first day of seventh grade at Willow Cove Middle School, Fiona thought *selkies* were simply mythological creatures. Then everything changed. She learned that she was a member of a small and very secret tribe of *selkies*, and with the help of her *selkie* cloak, she could change into a seal and rule the ocean.

Fiona often felt like she had two lives—one on land, one at sea.

As she often did, Fiona looked over the cliff's edge toward the ocean before going inside her house. It was a view she never tired of. Tonight the sun was a fiery ball reflecting on the waves, ranging from a deep crimson to a coppery red.

It's been too long since I've been in those waves, Fiona thought. But after all she'd just been through in New York City, when would she have time to go for a swim again?

Just as Fiona was thinking this, she caught sight of something familiar—a tuft of coppery-colored hair, just over by the sea. A passerby might have missed it, but not Fiona.

"Mom," Fiona said breathlessly.

A year ago Fiona would have never believed that her mom would be waiting for her by the sea cliffs. For a long time Fiona had believed her mother was dead. But her mother was, in fact, not dead. She was Queen Leana of the *selkies*. She had to live away from her daughter until Fiona was old enough to know the truth.

Fiona's mother sauntered up to her and embraced her daughter in a warm hug.

"Fiona," her mother said. Her voice was calm and relaxed, but Fiona could detect a slight panic in her mother's tremor. "Thank moonlight you are all right. So much has happened."

Fiona started to feel guilty. She'd only gone to New York to help a friend; she hadn't meant to worry her mother. She bit her lip.

"I'm sorry——" she started to say.

But it seemed Fiona's mother was worried about something else entirely.

"I'm afraid I have some troubling news," her mother said. "The *selkies* have learned that you've been foretold as one of the new First Four."

Fiona gasped. Her mind whirled with what-ifs. Through her mother, Fiona was *selkie* royalty. But the *selkies*' discovery of her role in the larger Changer world could spell disaster.

Fiona, along with her three friends—Mack Kimura, Darren Smith, and Gabriella Rivera—were foretold by an ancient prophecy to be the next leaders of the Changer world, the next First Four. Darren was an *impundulu*, a fearsome bird from southern Africa that could shoot lightning bolts from his razor-sharp talons and create violent storms. Gabriella could transform into a *nahual*, a jaguar with yellow eyes, sleek jet-black fur, and the ability to spirit-walk in other people's minds. And Makoto—Mack—was a *kitsune*, a powerful white fox with paws that blazed with fire. He had the ability to fly and to borrow other Changers' powers, just like his *kitsune* grandfather.

In their training, Fiona had learned that Changers once lived openly alongside humans. In fact, Changers did their best to protect humans from the world's dark forces. But the concept of real magic was too much for human brains to grasp. Thousands of years ago humans came to believe that Changers wanted to destroy them.

Fear is a strange thing. And fear—as fear does—made the humans act in strange, desperate ways. The Changers were forced to create a hidden world. They were still devoted to protecting humans from evil, but now they did so in secret—and from a distance.

Fiona, Darren, Mack, and Gabriella learned all of this in their training at the hands of the First Four, the current leaders of all Changer-kind.

Akira Kimura, Mack's grandfather, steered Fiona and her friends in the discovery and control of their new powers. Dorina Therian, a werewolf, was the kids' primary coach in their secretly enchanted gym at Willow Cove Middle School. Yara Moreno (an *encantado*, or dolphin Changer) and Sefu Badawi (a *bultungin*, or hyena Changer) stepped in to help every now and then.

From the moment Fiona first put on her *selkie* cloak and dove into the ocean waves, she felt more like herself than ever before. The rhythm and pulse of the tides were as natural to her as breathing. It was almost like . . . almost like she was *complete*.

But it was a world of deep divisions. The *selkie* faction, for instance, had a long-standing mistrust of the Changer nation. Fiona often felt torn between two *more* worlds, in addition her human one—her mother's *selkie* world and that of the Changer nation. Especially because, thanks to the prophecy and her lineage, Fiona was due to inherit both.

Bringing those two worlds together became even trickier when a new dark force came into play. An evil *kitsune* named Sakura Hiyamoto, or the Shadow Fox, had built an army to rise against the Changer nation. Sakura wanted control of everything—the magical *and* the nonmagical—and she was ready to go to war to get it.

What's more, the Shadow Fox was a memory eater. She could consume whatever memories she wanted, insert false memories, and absorb that Changer's powers. A former student of Mr. Kimura's, she had left him so she could delve into dark magic, and then Sakura turned on him, though Fiona didn't know why.

Sakura had long been underground, watching and waiting to take her revenge. But recently she had come out of hiding to amass her army—and her first target was Mack.

Mack—Fiona's friend. Mack—who was supposed to join them as the new First Four. Mack—who enjoyed making goofy faces and reading comic books.

Sakura had poisoned good, kind Mack's mind with dark magic and lured him in with promises of power. She replaced his memories of happiness and hope with those of anger and despair. Once that was complete, Mack was her pawn. He turned his back on the Changer nation and joined Sakura's dark forces.

But before they could rescue Mack, the First Four knew that Sakura would come after Fiona, Gabriella, and Darren next. Sakura would want the complete set. She was a collector, of sorts—of powerful Changers and their abilities—and wanted them in her army. Thankfully, Fiona was protected from Sakura's mind control with her powerful *selkie* Queen's Song, and Gabriella was protected by ancient Aztec magic in the form of the Ring of Tezcatlipoca. But Darren had no such shield. That's why the group had traveled to New York City: to lift an ancient curse and to find protection for him.

Before they could do that, however, Sakura's army had mounted a surprise attack. Many had been injured, but in the end the First Four and their followers prevailed—and one *very* good thing had come out of the battle. Gabriella had spirit-walked into Mack's mind and healed the pain that Sakura had inflicted. Their friend was himself again.

Gabriella had wanted Mack to come back home to Willow Cove with them, but Mack made a brave sacrifice instead. He chose to stay with Sakura as an agent for the First Four. Mack had mastered illusion magic and believed he could mask his true self from the evil master. His plan was to feed crucial inside information to the First Four, which could be the key to winning the war.

With war looming, Fiona and her mother had hoped the *selkies* would support the First Four. But it was a matter that required a gentle touch. Gaining that support required delicate and ongoing negotiations. Mother and daughter—queen and princess—had agreed that delicacy was only possible if Fiona's role as a member of the next First Four remain undisclosed.

But now those careful efforts had been ruined by the revelation of Fiona's secret.

Fiona was very right to be alarmed.

"The *selkies* are deeply divided about how to proceed," Fiona's mother said. "Many refuse to trust my leadership on this issue."

"How did they find out?" Fiona asked. "We've been so careful."

"I don't know," her mother answered. "There are some *selkies* who are sympathetic to Sakura's cause."

This made Fiona's stomach turn.

"Are *any selkies* on our side?" she asked.

"Some are," her mother answered. "There are those who feel comforted by the idea of a *selkie* as part of the next First Four, that leadership of the Changers will be returned to the *selkies* at last."

"But?" Fiona asked.

"But there is another *selkie* group, one that is actively undermining that belief. They're even calling into question my right to rule. They say that because I've known about the prophecy and kept it secret, that you and I are puppets of the First Four."

"But that's not true," Fiona said, her voice fading into a whisper. The word "puppet" felt like a wound to her heart. She had worked so hard to straddle those two realms, to learn everything she could about both the *selkies* and the larger Changer world. She had fought battles against evil forces and tried to get to know the needs of the various factions around her. She was *good*. She knew that. Why were people against her, still?

I'm exhausted, she thought. *All that effort, and now it's being met with lies and mistrust. It's not fair!*

"Of course it isn't true," her mother said. "You're nobody's puppet, nor am I. But this group is using that fear to try to convince the *selkies* that you're not really one of us—and that I'm not either."

Fiona took a deep breath and shook off her despair. *I've worked too hard to give up now,* she thought. Then she thought of Mack, who was *behind enemy lines.* Surely Mack had the hardest job of all. Suddenly, she didn't feel so bad for herself.

"What should we do?" she asked. "How can we make things better?"

"We must heal this division within the *selkie* faction before things get any worse. We don't need two wars on our hands," her mother said.

Fiona gasped. "*Two* wars? Do you mean the *selkies* would go to war with each other? A civil war?"

"I hope it won't go that far, but we must be sure it doesn't," her mother said. "So I've come up with a plan. You need to be more visible on the *selkie* isles. We'll move all your lessons there so the *selkies* learn you are loyal to our kind."

Fiona was about to object. The *selkies*' territory was a half day's swim from Willow Cove. *What if I'm needed in a battle with Sakura?* she worried.

"I know you want to stick close to the First Four," her mother said, as if reading her mind. "But your distance from the *selkie* isles is one of the biggest reasons why the *selkies* question your loyalty. You *must* strike up a friendship with some of the other youngling *selkies* and attend the next few council meetings. Let our people see that you're interested and trustworthy. It'll make all the difference. We're just a proud group—we don't want to be run by outsiders. I know they will come to love you as I love you."

Fiona bit her lip, not sure how to respond. Darren, Gabriella, and Mack needed her. And what would her father do? He could barely boil pasta for himself! She knew her mother wouldn't ask her lightly to leave everyone, but so far her relationship with the other *selkies* hadn't exactly been rosy. Some *selkies* had actually made fun of her in a council meeting; others ignored her entirely.

But then another thought occurred to her. *If I really am going to be a leader one day, then I must try to unite the selkies—and perhaps with the Changer nation, too.*

Fiona was about to agree to the journey when her mother added a condition.

"As you can understand, this situation is dire," her mother said. "As such, you cannot share where you're going with your friends or with the First Four."

More secrets?

Fiona was apt to protest—surely she had to tell the First Four where she was going. Yes, she'd be with her mother, but—but—

Fiona lost track of her thoughts. Out of the corner of her eye, way into town, she spotted a massive lightning storm forming in the distance. Fiona looked out. She knew where that lightning was coming from. It was in the direction of Darren's house.

Something's wrong, Fiona thought, *Darren wouldn't create a storm like that. Not unless he was in danger . . .*

"Fiona?" Queen Leana asked, staring at her daughter. "Fiona, do you understand me?"

Fiona took another glance at the lightning storm.

"I'm sorry, Mom, I really am," she said. "But I—I have to go."

Darren stood in the entrance to his family room, watching lightning zigzag up and down his older brother Ray's arms. It was impossible, almost, that his brother could suddenly wield lightning—Darren had thought he was the only *impundulu* in the family—but it was happening nonetheless.

"Darren, stay back!" Ray yelled.

Darren could see the fear in his brother's eyes. The same fear Darren had experienced when he first came into his powers. He had no idea what was happening and, like Ray, had no control over this bizarre new power.

Darren drew his hands together and called on his

own powers to create a ball of counterelectricity. Then he moved his hands apart to make a circle, forming a force field around the two of them. Even though lightning still emanated from Ray's fingertips, he no longer could damage anything—or, more importantly, *anyone*.

Could it be? Darren thought. Was the curse he'd meant to break in New York City lifted? If his brother suddenly had lightning powers, surely that meant the curse was lifted, that Darren's Changer bloodline was coming into their powers again, that Ray was an *impundulu* too—

And if Ray was an *impundulu*, the curse *had* to have been lifted. The Spider's Curse—which Darren had recently learned was pressed upon his family generations ago—made sure that no *impundulus* in their bloodline came to power. Somehow, Darren's powers managed to emerge, anyway.

In ancient times a bitter conflict had erupted between the spider Changers, the *anansis*, and the *impundulus* for control of a strategic region in Southwest Africa. During the conflict the *anansis* had cursed many *impundulus* with a powerful poison contained in their bite. The curse was passed down from generation to generation and prevented all but the most powerful *impundulus* from being able to transform and discover their Changer gifts.

Darren was one of those powerful *impundulus*, but he had no older family members who were Changers. No one to help guide him in those difficult and confusing early days.

Even worse, because of that curse, Darren was also unable to benefit from a protection spell that would keep him safe from Sakura's mind control. So he and the others had flown to New York by *tengu*, a bird that commanded the wind and could transport anyone anywhere in the blink of an eye, to meet the descendant of the *anansi* who had cursed his ancestor. If the *anansi* agreed to forgive his bloodline, Darren had believed he could be protected from Sakura with an ancient spell.

Unfortunately, although Esi Akosua, the young *anansi* in question, was willing to forgive Darren, she didn't believe that would change anything for him. She had offered forgiveness to other *impundulus* her ancestors had bitten, yet the curse had remained in place.

Darren tried to think back. Had Esi forgiven him

in some different way? Perhaps the fact they hid from Sakura together made her really *mean* the forgiveness. That could certainly explain everything!

While things were coming clear for Darren, Ray was still mystified.

Ray stared at his little brother openmouthed. Darren was wielding the same kind of electrical power that was exploding from his own fingertips, and doing a much better job of it.

"You—you can—*what?*" Ray stammered.

"Er, you might want to calm down," Darren said. But Ray didn't calm down. The lightning in Ray's palms became more unstable. "Ray, you have to calm down or it won't stop."

"'Calm down'?" Ray yelled. "What do you mean calm down? There's *lightning* running up and down my arms. I can't calm down! What's happening?"

How many times had Darren imagined this conversation? Wished that his older brother were an *impundulu* too? But in every one of those scenarios, Ray was helping *him* out, not the other way around. Darren wasn't sure what to say. He swallowed.

"You're an *impundulu*—a magical shape-shifting bird—and so am I."

Ray shook his head. "You're hallucinating. We must both be hallucinating."

"No, we're Changers," Darren said. He started to ramble. "I found out on the first day of school. It runs in families, and I thought I was the only one in our family, but then I found out there was a curse that blocked your powers, I guess, and Esi said it wouldn't work, but it did, and now you're one of us, and . . ."

Darren stopped and took a deep breath, but Ray didn't look any less scared and confused than he had a minute ago. There were still sparks crackling from the tips of his fingers.

"What's an Esi? What are you talking about?" Ray demanded.

I'm no good at explaining this, Darren thought. He had so longed for a family member, especially Ray, to share this new world with. He had just never thought about having to be the one to explain it all. *I need to get in touch with Ms. Therian. If anyone knows how to explain this—and how to keep Ray in check—it's her,* he thought.

Darren was about to call Ms. Therian when the front door slammed open.

Please don't be Mom, he thought over and over again. He didn't want to explain to his mom why her kids were suddenly enveloped in a lightning storm.

"Darren? Darren?" came a voice.

Darren recognized that voice. Thankfully, it wasn't his mom at all—it was Fiona!

For a brief second Darren was happy to hear her, but that was soon replaced with a new worry. *I don't know if I can hold the force field much longer,* Darren worried. *Fiona could accidentally get hurt.*

"Fiona!" Darren shouted back. "It's not safe. Call Ms. Therian."

"Fiona?" Ray repeated. "Your friend from school? Oh, don't tell me she's an *impun*—"

Ray's question was cut off by Fiona herself, soaking wet from the storm that raged over their house. She wove a water shield around herself and took a look at Ray.

"Is Ray . . . ?" Fiona asked.

"Yes," Darren said.

"So the curse is . . ."

"Broken."

There was a beat of silence. Then Fiona's face brightened.

"Professor Zwane can work the protection spell now, Darren," she said earnestly. "You'll be protected from Sakura!"

"Yes, that's great," Darren said, "but right now we need to get Ms. Therian. Ray needs her help."

Fiona dropped her water shield and pulled out her cell phone. She dialed Mrs. Therian, but there was no answer. Then she dialed again. Still no answer.

"She's always by her phone," Fiona said. "Where could she be?"

An exhausted Darren dropped his guard for a second, and that was all it took. Ray's powers were too unwieldy to control. A stray bolt of lightning burst from Ray's fingertips and zipped past Darren—right to Fiona.

"Ack!" Fiona screamed.

It all happened in an instant.

Fire. Something smelled like fire. The room was covered in yellow light and then darkened into black. For a brief pause no lightning emanated from Ray. It was like the world froze still.

"Fiona!" Darren yelled.

Was she hurt? Darren could barely see her—all he could *smell* was ash. Like something—or rather, some-*one*—had just been burned.

Thankfully, he heard Fiona's voice.

"I'm . . . okay," Fiona replied breathlessly.

Whew. Fiona was already working on putting out the fire with water when Darren noticed what Ray had hit. It was Fiona's hair! Fiona's hair was completely buzzed on one side. For a moment he was scared, but then he couldn't help but think it looked, well, *cool.*

But there was more where that came from. Lightning ping-ponged from the wall to the ceiling and back again.

"I'm sorry! I'm so sorry!" Ray kept yelling, doing his best to cover up his hands, but the lightning just wouldn't stop. With each "sorry," another jolt came out.

Fiona ducked into the hall to try calling Ms. Therian again while Darren worked on building a new—and hopefully, more durable—force field. The smell of singed hair filled his nostrils.

Darren remembered the time he almost killed Fiona in the ancillary gym where they had their Changer training. He had shot a lightning arrow that missed its mark, shattered an overhead light, and nearly fell into the saltwater pool where Fiona was training. It missed by less than an inch—and Darren felt *terrible*.

Thankfully, he'd had Ms. Therian's help then. Darren knew he needed her help again now, more than anything.

Fiona kept calling and calling, but there was no response. It was so unlike Ms. Therian. Fiona tried a few other numbers, but nothing seemed to work.

Darren didn't know what was going on.

Where are you, Ms. Therian? Darren wondered.

Looking for another great book?
Find it
IN THE MIDDLE.

Fun, fantastic books for kids
in the in-be**TWEEN** age.

IntheMiddleBooks.com